SHORT STORY INTERNATIONAL

**Tales by the World's
Great Contemporary Writers
Presented Unabridged**

All selections in
Short Story International
are published full and
unabridged.

Editor
Sylvia Tankel

Associate Editor
Erik Sandberg-Diment

Contributing Editor
John Harr

Assistant Editors
Mildred Butterworth
Debbie Kaufman
Kirsten Hammerle

Art Director
Carol Anderson

Circulation Director
Nat Raboy

Production Director
Michael Jeffries

Business Manager
John O'Connor

Publisher
Sam Tankel

Volume 17, Number 98, June 1993.
Short Story International (USPS 375-970)
Copyright © by International Cultural
Exchange 1993. Printed in U.S.A. All rights
reserved. Reproduction in whole or in part
prohibited. Second class postage paid at
Great Neck, N.Y. 11022 and at additional
mailing offices. **Editorial offices: P.O. Box
405, Great Neck, N.Y. 11022.** Enclose
stamped, self-addressed envelope with
submission. One year (six issues) subscription
for U.S., U.S. possessions $24, Canada $27
(US), other countries $29 (US). Single copy
price $5.75 (US). **For subscriptions and
address changes write to *Short Story
International*, P.O. Box 405, Great
Neck, N.Y. 11022.** *Short Story
International* is published bimonthly by
International Cultural Exchange, 6 Sheffield
Road, Great Neck, N.Y. 11021. Postmaster:
please send address changes to *Short Story
International*, P.O. Box 405, Great Neck,
N.Y. 11022.

Table of Contents

Copyrights
and acknowledgments

We wish to express deep thanks to the authors, publishers, translators and literary agents for their permission to publish the stories in this issue.

"The Decision" by Margot Titcher. Copyright Margot Titcher. "Thorn in the Flesh" by Eric Cameron appeared in *Portland Monthly.* Copyright Eric Cameron. "Fine Moon" by Chi Li appeared in *Chinese Literature*, 1991. Translation by Wang Ying. By permission. "Bricks" by Josip Novakovich appeared in *Prairie Schooner*, 1992. Copyright Josip Novakovich. "The Bath" from Kypria Epi by Panos Ioannides. Translation by David Bailey. Copyright Panos Ioannides. "Complete Destruction, Absolute Disaster" by John Haylock. Copyright 1993 John Haylock. "Milkmoney" by Mehrdad Nabili, 1993. "Encounter" by Shammai Golan appeared in *Signals*, ed. Alan Ross. Copyright Shammai Golan. "Your Son and Ideals" from *Honour and Other Stories* by Goh Sin Tub. Published by Reed International (Singapore) Pte Ltd. Copyright 1986 Goh Sin Tub. "Showdown at Horton's" from *Gece Vardiyasi* by Fakir Baykurt. Translation by Joseph S. Jacobson, 1993. "Feast of Love" by Todd Rolf Zeiss, 1992. "Charity, Goddess of Our Day" from *False Gods* by Louis Auchincloss. Copyright © 1992 Louis Auchincloss. By permission of Houghton Mifflin Company and Curtis Brown Ltd. "Life Game" by Uyen Loewald, 1993.

Photo credits: Louis Auchincloss by Frank E. Schramm.

"Don't say a word till I'm done, or my nerve
is sure to desert me."

The Decision

BY MARGOT TITCHER

THE car park's gravel crunched noisily beneath the wheels of the chair. It was the only sound in the still, hot air apart from the bell.

The cheerful chiming rose to the crowns of the surrounding eucalypts; it drifted across the valley, over cultivated farmlands, to lose itself in the distant mountain range, the resonant notes reducing to a mere bellbird's tink.

From within the weatherboard church—the gleaming white exterior a testament to the fervor of a recent working-bee—the ancient organ wheezed into life.

"What are you doing? You're going in the wrong direction."

The querulous rebuke brought Myrtle's attention to the present. Her mother was right, not that she'd admit it to her. In her distraction, Myrtle had been steering the chair towards the front steps when she knew perfectly well she'd need the ground level access at the transept door, slipping into an old habit, back to the days when Dad was alive.

By the time she maneuvered the invalid into the nearest pew and folded the wheelchair, the congregation was in full voice. A surplice-clad choirboy slid into position alongside his fellows, while out in the corrugated iron bell-shed the bellrope still jiggled wildly from his final tug.

When those who were able, among the ageing membership, knelt for the first prayer, Myrtle mumbled to her mother and tiptoed from the building—words deliberately indistinct, guaranteed to exasperate her partially-deaf parent.

"Why didn't you go before we left home?" Myrtle heard her say, and hoped the query was inaudible to the parishioners in the body of the church.

But stepping out into the bright sunlight she knew she didn't really care. Not today. Not ever again.

Myrtle smiled as she drove, wondering what the Nosy Parker neighbors would make of her premature return home, her Sunday routine so inveterate the slightest deviation was certain to be remarked upon.

However, most blinds were drawn against the heat and not a curtain stirred when, the engine idling, she dragged the suitcase out from under the privet hedge, tossed It into the passenger seat, climbed in behind the wheel and continued along the road out of town.

The bitumen surface extended only to the last of the shops. The businesses had all seen better days. All closed at the moment in deference to the Sabbath, a number were permanently shuttered. Several verandahs were sorely in need of repair and none of the structures had received a coat of paint since the highway had been put in, bypassing the small settlement.

Perhaps someday it would become a curiosity, a classic example of a bygone lifestyle, encapsulated, attracting tourists from around the state. Well, I for one won't be around to witness it, thought Myrtle.

She pulled up opposite Bellamys' Ladieswear. She wanted to savor the memory of yesterday morning.

Eyes shut, she fancied she could hear again the dialogue from the point where Thelma, leaning across the counter, had confided,

"Guess who's back in town? Russ! Russ Harman!

"And he's been inquiring about you. Whether you were still living locally. Whether your mother was still alive. He's still a bit of a dasher, going gray at the sides, but then, most of our old class turn forty this year. I'm going to hate it. What about you?"

"Tell me more about Russ."

"Well...he's much thinner. And sadder, somehow. You know how he was always good for a laugh. Well, he smiles, but not with his eyes.

"His wife died, he said, sometime last year. S'pose he's worried about the kids; the youngest's only eight. I didn't like to ask what she died from, the wife. He married one of his cousins, didn't he? Anyway, he'll probably tell you all about it. Said he was heading for your place. He's only here for the weekend.

"When he talked about you...I can't explain...he went sort of...soft. I bet he's come back for you, Myrtle. I bet he has. He's sure to be thinking of marrying again. He must be lonely in the outback without a partner. And he'll need help with the youngsters. Besides, he never looked at anyone else when you were around. We were all so jealous."

That was true; it was universally acknowledged that they were "meant for each other." Automatically, they were paired at parties, and tennis matches, and picnics down by the river. Myrtle recalled the protracted embraces when he and she dropped behind the group on the moonlight paperchase, and at the dance in the decorated scout hall when the generator failed. They had not "overstepped the mark," they could afford to wait, time was on their side. Anticipation had heightened their awareness of one another and, although it was their stated aim to earn the town's blessing by keeping life's events in the approved chronological order, on occasions their resolve came close to weakening.

Remembering, Myrtle felt a warmth suffusing her body. She studied her reflection in the rear-view mirror. Why, with her flushed cheeks she almost appeared youthful again. A quick tug at the bobby pins, and her hair, till now disciplined in a style encouraged by Mother, fell to her shoulders. She could be mistaken for that twenty-two-year-old, provided nobody examined her intently. But would he? Would he hold her at arms length and scrutinize the face, the no-longer-willowy figure? No, of course not: they would be hugging. Time for talking, for filling in the years, later.

It was pure chance she had come into the shops on Saturday, on yet another errand for Mother to exchange something. Nothing Myrtle purchased pleased her mother, be it an item of clothing, footwear, napery or kitchenware. Everything was either too bright, too tight, too short, or not a brand she favored. Sometimes she was more subtle. "It's not what I wanted," she'd say, "but it'll do, after all it's *only* for me." All this with such exaggerated resignation that Myrtle would seize the offending article and insist, herself, that it must go back.

"Sorry, Thelma, she doesn't like it. No, that's not strictly true. She *likes* the dress, but do you have it in blue? I swear it seems I've changed more things for that woman than I've bought in the first place."

But what Thelma had to say that morning had put everything else out of her mind.

"I'll just say you don't have another color," Myrtle had said. "If you do, I don't want to know," she'd added, heading for the door.

She had been on foot. Mother didn't like her to use the car. It was "a waste of petrol, besides you are fit, not like your poor old mother." Myrtle was skilled at mimicking her mother's words.

Normally, she wouldn't have minded the walk. In fact, she would have dawdled, enjoying the sunshine and her own company, not relishing the demands on her time and patience waiting back at the house.

On her return it would be the plaintive "Myrtle, is that you?" and "Myrtle?" in the familiar, singsong whine, whenever she sat at the piano or opened a book.

Myrtle's personal enthusiasms and opinions ranked low on Mother's scale of importance. Conversation consisted of Mother's incessant ramblings about places and people mainly unknown to Myrtle. She listened with a contrived expression of attentiveness, confident that she could contribute when pressed, repetition having etched the anecdotes onto her memory—tales of Mother's former acquaintances, and of Aunt Pansy and Aunt Marigold who had wangled more than their share of the family's goods, and on and on.

Pansy and Marigold. What names! Her own was little better. She was named by Mother after a great-aunt, in anticipation that flattery would ensure a mention in the ageing female's will; in the event, Myrtle reflected ruefully, she, Myrtle, had been saddled with an anachronistic label, while the elderly maiden had bequeathed her all to a Lost Dogs' Home.

Myrtle's older sister had escaped the botanic bias with *Matilda* in honor of her paternal grandmother, a name soon contracted to Tilly, which Myrtle considered particularly apt. It somehow bespoke her character: Silly Tilly, Frilly Tilly, Trilly Tilly.

Myrtle wondered, now, how Tilly would react to her unwanted responsibility. And their brother Arthur?

Well, that was their problem; she'd done her share—and more. She'd been penalized for being single. A life sentence, and for what crime?

Myrtle had entered the house with a "Thelma doesn't have it in blue, she'll arrange a credit."

"I would have kept the green, then."

"It's too late. Want a cuppa?"

"If you won't go back and get the green dress for me, I'll have to ask one of the neighbors."

Identifying a well-known ploy, Myrtle refused to rise to the bait. "Suit yourself. I've put the sugar in."

"Russ Harman called in. You've just missed him."

"Why didn't you say? Thelma said he was in town."

"Yes, he's come back to settle his parents into that new Hostel for the Aged at the edge of town, and to put their farm on the market. He's selling through Reagan's Real Estate where you used to work."

"Did he leave a message for me?"

"No."

"He didn't even *mention* me?"

"I didn't say that. I said there's no message."

"Well, what did he say about me, then?"

"Nothing much. He asked whether you were still living with

me. 'Where else would she be,' I said to him, 'with me so incapacitated?'"

"And that was all you talked about?"

"Oh no, but nothing more about you. He asked had I ever considered living with Arthur and Bea, or with Tilly and her family. I told him I wouldn't dream of burdening them, and why should I when I had you to fetch and carry for me. Then he went on about his parents and how happy they were to be going to the hostel, and had I seen it, and the nursing home on the same grounds. I said you wouldn't catch me dead in one of those places and that I intended to see my days out right here where I belong."

It was then that Myrtle made her decision. She was surprised how easy it was. She would go to the Harman farm; she would tell Russ that Mother's needs would not separate them—not again, not now Fate had granted them this second chance.

Vividly, she recollected that other occasion: Dad, barely in his grave; Russ, going interstate to manage his widowed cousin's outback property and begging Myrtle to accompany him; Mother, histrionically declaring she didn't know what her dear husband would have said about his wife being left alone, and she not in the best of health; Arthur and Bea, leaving hurriedly; and Silly Tilly, pleading her belly, and a toddler already beside her.

For approximately eighteen months she and Russ had corresponded. But it was awkward, what with Mother asking to be read his letters and Myrtle conscious that Russ continued to feel slighted. She had learned third-hand of his marriage to his widowed relative, then the letters had stopped.

Myrtle wished she had owned shoes other than *sensible* ones to pack. And some pretty jewelry. Mother had handed down, apart from her rings and the odd favorite piece, all the family jewelry to Tilly. Confronted with Myrtle's indignation, she had justified the action by pointing out that Tilly had daughters to pass them on to. Myrtle had stormed into her bedroom, the only room she wasn't obliged to share, and shouted into her pillow that it wasn't *her* fault she had no family of her own—no Russ, no children.

Was it too late now? Women were producing at thirty-nine. Maybe more rare, more risky, with a first pregnancy, but not unheard of. Surely the Good Lord would look favorably upon two, no longer star-crossed mortals.

A throb of yearning started up somewhere deep inside her, and a rush of sensuous imaginings of the kind she was used to suppressing but today gave free rein to. A voice, barely recognizable as her own, was repeating, "Russ! Russ!"

A family of her own. It was only last week when Mother began her usual "I might as well be dead" or "I won't see another summer," or whatever variation on the timeworn theme she had been playing to elicit sympathy, that Myrtle had snapped: "Stop grizzling! You'll always be better off than I. You've got something I won't have when I'm your age."

Disbelief had diverted Mother, temporarily, from further indulgence in introversion. In her deplorable state, how could she be the object of another's envy?

"What have I got that you won't have?"

Myrtle rounded on her heel and walked from the room, tossing the answer over her shoulder as she left.

"A Myrtle, that's what."

But now, that was all to alter. She'd have her own family, after all—husband, stepchildren, and perhaps even the baby. Myrtle hugged herself, mentally.

In reality, she was concentrating on the road. The bitumen had petered out, its place taken by corduroy ridges, potholes, and the ever-present dust—talcum fine and penetrating, it insinuated itself into the car's interior despite the tightly-closed windows, depositing its pale film on every surface.

Myrtle changed gear as the road climbed sharply. Partway up the rise, she swung the wheel to the left and drove into the little cemetery. It was merely a patch of scrub with headstones dotted through it—no pathways, no order—but Dad always said his soul could rest nowhere else, that he had more relatives here than in any other spot in the world. He would have none of the clipped lawns, the paving, the geometric precision of the new cemetery to the west of town.

Myrtle shared Dad's affection for the bush. Here, there was a triumph of nature over a harsh environment, a wild beauty—a wild beauty enhanced in springtime by the countless spikes of pink and red native heath. Independent, dignified, yet undeniably delicate with a profusion of exquisite bells—small wonder they were Myrtle's favorite flower.

The heat was becoming oppressive. Faced with the sun's intense rays, the eucalypts drooped their narrow leaves out of a sense of self-preservation, withdrawing their protective shade from the creatures moving about their roots, be they the odd lizard, a colony of frenetic bullants, or a lone human conversing with her father.

"Dad, I've something to tell you. Don't say a word till I'm done, or my nerve is sure to desert me.

"Dad, Russ's back. I'm on my way to him right now. Then I'm going with him to the outback. Be happy for me, please.

"I know I promised you. But deathbed promises are not binding, you know. When you stared out at me through your pain and said, 'Look after your mother, Myrtle,' what could I say?

"I was too young, too inexperienced to know what it entailed.

"Why only me? Arthur and Tilly got off scot free. Anyway, they'll have to pull their weight, now.

"Neither of them will do a stint the length of the one I've just completed, so they'll still be ahead.

"I intended to carry on, you know. But Russ needs me, and so do his children. And my need? It's so overwhelming, so precious, I can't put it into words, even to you.

"You're worrying about Mother, aren't you? Well, she's in a wheelchair now, but the doctor said she brought it on herself. Had she followed his advice and kept more active, her arthritis would be less advanced, her weight less, and her muscles more capable. Just sitting around feeling sorry for herself and complaining, and doing nothing for herself, was her own choice.

"She's always making me miserable with her, 'I've got nothing to live for.'

"Dad, *I* do have something to live for, at last, and I won't let anything stop me.

"Make it easier for me. Tell me you understand. Give me your blessing.

"O.K. It's your turn. I'm finished."

Myrtle gazed at the headstone, at the space left to add "and his loving wife Ivy" and at the allowance for "and their beloved daughter Myrtle." She had cheated them. She would lie with Russ forever now: in life and death.

"Well?" she said.

His voice was clear. He could have been standing at her elbow. There was no doubt it was he—the same firm, yet gentle, tone he'd always adopted with her.

"Myrtle, you must go back home."

"No...o...o! Her anguished shriek sent a crow, from his perch on a branch above her, flapping slowly, mournfully, to a position of greater safety—a silent witness to her distress, its plumage the black of widows' weeds.

"Dad! You can't *do* this to me. It's not fair!" She raged around the grave. Under her feet shed twigs snapped loudly as she stamped. She knelt down and beat clenched fists on the ground in front of her to make the deceased, six feet below the surface, take heed, bend to her will. Her tears trickling onto the parched soil were instantly absorbed. The searing sun striking her head caused her to feel slightly faint.

Myrtle subsided onto her heels.

He spoke again. Or was it all in her mind, she questioned.

"Myrtle." The voice less firm, sorrowful. "You *must* go back."

She returned to the car, her feet dragging, her shoulders slumped—a study of dejection. Whether Dad had, in fact, directed her was immaterial; she was broken, her determination diluted, her own desires subjugated.

"I'm not doing it for you, Mother," she said, putting the key into the ignition. "But I will do it for Dad. For what he and I once had. To stop him fretting about you. To give him peace.

"But I won't ever feel the same about him. The resentment will always be between us. I asked, and he refused me. He asked, and I complied. It's just not fair. It's never been fair. How could you, Dad? What about *me*?"

Half an hour late. The vicar must be frantic, thought Myrtle. It was one thing to be saying unctuously, "Your mother is such a fine woman, so affable, so outgoing, so accepting of her lot," and another to find yourself wholly responsible for her.

How do *you* like it, Vicar? Wondering what you'll do if Myrtle—good old Myrtle, ever-reliable Myrtle—maybe, just maybe, doesn't show up? Suddenly your own pursuits take second place, don't they, eh? You can't take the narrow dirt track to the vicarage, can you? Not until Mother's well-being is determined. What about your midday roast? Spoiling? Wife impatient? Even long-suffering, vicar's wives like meals on time. Apprehensive about your reception when you materialize with an elderly parishioner in tow? What then? Offer accommodation for the night? Scurry around town in a desperate search for someone with knowledge of the next-of-kin, so you can unload her posthaste? What! You don't want a "fine" woman underfoot? "Fine?" Try peevish, obstinate, demanding. Think about it, Vicar. Not quite the same without Myrtle, is it?

Myrtle regretted having unfastened her hair; her neck had become damp and sticky. Ruefully, she eyed her scuffed shoes and brushed soil from the front of her frock.

Nearing the church, she spotted them by the roadside—the two of them: the vicar, flustered, standing mute behind the chair, trite conversation long since expended, his ecclesiastical garments so appropriate before the altar strangely incongruent in the harsh sunlight, grass seeds decorating the hem, the perspiration beading his forehead and rosy scalp not altogether due to the temperature; and Mother, her expression alternating between indignation and consternation.

The couple caught sight of the car, simultaneously.

Myrtle smiled in spite of herself. What a picture she must present—disheveled, red-eyed. She would have extracted a degree of perverse enjoyment from the discomfort she had caused, had she not felt so withered inside, so...spent.

She must keep herself in check until she could be alone tonight. God help these two should either say the wrong thing to her.

But the vicar was too relieved to inquire into her vanishing. He made his good-byes with dispatch and hurried in the direction of the cooking aromas.

Mother's "Tut!" at the sight of her daughter's condition died on her lips when she read the comment-if-you-dare message in Myrtle's face. She settled for a glare, as Myrtle assisted her into the back seat and stowed the folded chair into the boot. And they had traveled some distance before she spoke.

"Anyway, Myrtle, it serves you right."

"What serves me right?"

"Russ Harman arrived at the church right after you left."

"Russ?" Myrtle, close to tears stiffened her body, willing herself to show no reaction.

"Yes. He came with his new bride-to-be. Introduced her to all and sundry after the service."

Ye gods! She'd come within a hair's breadth of making an absolute idiot of herself.

Understanding came quickly. "Thank you, Dad," she said out loud. "Thank you."

"What did you say?"

"Nothing."

"You did so. I heard you."

"Oh, shut up, Mother. Just appreciate the view."

Born in 1933, in Victoria, Margot Titcher taught primary school until her marriage. She has been writing since 1973 and her stories have been published in Australia, New Zealand and the USA. Mrs. Titcher has won several prizes in short story contests, including the Nambucca Heads Bicentennial Literary Competition in 1988. In 1992 "The Decision" won the Grenfell (N.S.W.) Henry Lawson Short Story Award. Genealogical research and photography are among her prime interests. Her story "The Letter" appeared in SSI No. 84.

"...whatever we do get for it will be untaxable capital gain."

Thorn in the Flesh

BY ERIC CAMERON

SLUMPED in the depths of a bulging, blackleather armchair near his second-floor bedroom window, Henry Morris watched the gradual transition from night to day. His old cottage, perched near the edge of a steep bluff, commanded a sweeping view of the river estuary and the sea beyond. Its gray roof and white shingled sides gave it the appearance of a well-fed sea gull at rest.

Needing little sleep, the old man liked to pass the hours of darkness with the warm, glowing eye of his pipe bowl kindling memories of happier times before the death of his wife. He sniffed the pungent smell of the coarse-cut tobacco and made a note to air the room before Gladys and his son, Peter, got up. His domineering daughter-in-law had made it known in no uncertain terms that she had a marked aversion to pipe smoke.

One of these days, Henry reminded himself, he would have to make an effort and stand up for his rights in his own home. First, though, he would have to devise some way of contending with

Gladys. Never underestimate the power of the female, he thought wryly, wondering how Peter had come to fall in love with such a thorn in the flesh. During the four years since Gladys and Peter had moved in with him, Henry Morris had learned that she was someone you opposed at your peril.

There were times when Henry wished that he had run away as a young man, instead of working his way from office boy to bookkeeper for Ross & Crandall, Ship Chandlers. He would imagine himself in a captain's uniform, braced on the swaying bridge of a trim freighter knifing through tropic seas to Hong Kong and other exotic ports of call. The closest he ever came to it was his weekly ferry ride across the harbor, a Sunday afternoon treat when the weather was good.

Yet, from middle age on, Henry Morris could have passed himself off as a grizzled mariner. Years of gardening and puttering along the beach had given his large-boned features the ruddy, wind-whipped look of a seafaring man. A deceptively gruff voice and stern blue eyes shadowed by beetling eyebrows completed the camouflage for a mild, almost timid nature. In the firm he had become known as a "soft touch" when it came to obtaining money with a hard-luck story. Even his own son now took advantage of him, never offering a penny toward the taxes and constant expenses required to keep the old house shipshape. He and Gladys seemed to consider that her housekeeping, haphazard as it was, was contribution enough. Until he learned to eat her cooking with caution, the old man had suffered from chronic heartburn.

Sensing a slight vibration underfoot, Henry cocked a wary eye toward the bedroom door, even though it was much too early for the others to be up and about. It probably was ground tremors from some construction project in the mountains that formed a striking, snow-capped backdrop to the harbor basin.

Henry's shyness was partly to blame for the lack of communication with his pliant and impressionable son. They had never had any common interests. An ardent sport fisherman when he was more active, Henry Morris had hoped that he and Peter would go off on trips together to fish for salmon and trout. But Peter had scorned the sport as a waste of time and had gone to the movies as often as he could beg or borrow the money. His present ambition as a junior stock and bond salesman was to make as much money as he could in as short a time as possible. So far, he had lost more than half of his father's carefully saved rainy day fund on what he had been convinced was a "sure thing." But the mining issue had been inflated by heavy promotion, and when the promoters pulled out their support it had sunk to a level from which it had never recovered. Henry sighed whenever he thought of the ornate stock certificate in his bank safety deposit box.

Gladys could have done much better than Peter in the world of finance, he was convinced. Her computer-like facility with facts and figures always made him feel inadequate. The truth was that he felt ashamed that he, a bookkeeper for most of his working years, was no match for a slim, self-possessed young woman in whose inscrutable dark eyes he thought he sometimes detected a flicker of sardonic disdain.

For all her intelligence, Gladys merely stayed at home to read and listen to her collection of classical records that was slowly spreading around the living room like some creeping black fungus growth. Her occasional forays into fashionable, expensive little boutiques invariably resulted in arguments with Peter about money...arguments that Gladys could win without once giving way to emotion. Henry was puzzled and a little disturbed by the realization that he had never seen his daughter-in-law cry. The closest she came to it was a strained expression, like someone in a dentist's chair expecting the drill to strike a nerve.

As the rising sun flowed over the rim of the hills its rays gilded the tall office buildings across the river, then flowed down to set a million brilliant eyes blinking on the water's surface. From the narrow, shingle beach at the foot of the bluff arose a moist odor of decaying flotsam deposited by the tides. With a slight pang, Henry recalled his wife's collection of oddly contorted pieces of driftwood. On his last salmon fishing excursion up the coast one weekend, Gladys had taken the opportunity to consign the wood to the fireplace.

After airing the bedroom and getting dressed, Henry crept down to the kitchen to have a slice of toast and a glass of orange juice before Gladys and Peter stirred. Then he went down to the beach, slowly picking his way along the narrow path that zig-zagged between the old fir trees clinging to the steep slope. Now and then he paused to listen to a new sound, finally identifying it as the chuckling, gurgling noise made by water flowing underground, the run-off of a recent spell of unusually heavy rains.

Reaching the water's edge, Henry startled a flock of herring gulls that rose in fluttering disorder, like the thoughts winging through his troubled mind. The gulls had been at the bedraggled carcass of an adult bald eagle. The once-majestic bird of prey lay soiled with a scum of diesel oil, the fierce golden eyes now gone from the sockets.

The eagles nested in a centuries-old fir tree not far from the cottage. Bitter anger stirred in Henry as he wondered whether some callous youth with a rifle had brought the eagle plunging from the sky. Or had the bird perhaps succumbed to old age? He would miss its harsh, keening cry as it wheeled in graceful spirals over the river.

All too soon the sky became overcast and a fine drizzle shrouded the hills. Henry buttoned his tweed jacket and started back to the cottage. The woods now were as somber as a ruined cathedral, while a sinister-sounding wind ghosted through the treetops. He had the eerie feeling that he was not alone, that some unseen thing slipped quietly from tree trunk to tree trunk in the gloom, always just behind him yet always out of sight whenever he glanced back.

The southeaster was driving a mean, chopping gray sea up the estuary as he reached the house. Entering very quietly, Henry eased the back door shut against the wind's insolent thrust and paused to catch his breath. Then he overheard Gladys and Peter in the dining room.

"This old house won't be all that easy to sell," Peter said.

"Paint can cover up a lot of things," Gladys countered. "And anyway, whatever we do get for it will be untaxable capital gain."

"It's liable to collapse before that day comes."

"Eight months or so isn't such a long time," Gladys objected. "Dr. Fowler said this could easily be his last summer."

"Are you serious?" Peter sounded startled.

"His heart could give out any time."

"And you let him go up and down that steep path to the beach?"

Gladys countered coolly. "Why deprive him of the only pleasure he seems to have left? He doesn't have a heart condition, but at his age anything could happen." She sounded to Henry like a lecturer. "My father died suddenly in his sleep. Mother didn't even know until she tried to wake him. Sometimes I think I'll walk into that smelly back bedroom and go over to the old armchair and find—"

"Never mind," Peter hastily interrupted. "I'm late. Have a meeting with the new director. I'll have to play my cards right this time."

Henry Morris tiptoed up the back stairway and gained the refuge of his room unseen. He sank into the big armchair with a sigh of relief. Closing his eyes, he listened to the rain spitting against the window like grains of sand. The wind swooped at the shingles like some hungry beast of prey trying to claw its way into the house. Peter's car roared in the drive, then faded away with a grinding of gears. Gladys drove much better than her husband.

So this was the way a life ended, Henry reflected. It was like reading a book late in the afternoon and not noticing the failing light. You paused and looked up to find the light almost gone. Looking down again at the book you found the printed page a pale, meaningless blur.

As the drumming of rain on the roof increased to a steady roar, the downpour became so heavy that it blotted out the view of white-maned waves charging up the river. When the house gave a long shudder Henry tensed expectantly. The strange quivering went through all the timbers once more, as if the building was gathering itself to flee from some impending danger.

From just below the rim of the bluff there came a sullen, muffled rumble accompanied by a crackling of timber that sounded like a scattered volley of rifle fire. Then half the garden suddenly detached itself and sank slowly and majestically out of sight. The house trembled.

Gladys rushed out and stood transfixed. Then she turned to look at the house.

Henry was taken aback by the proprietary expression on her face. Believing that he had been buried by the clay slide, Gladys was already taking quick stock of her property. But she was unaware of the swiftly widening crack in the ground just behind her.

Leaning close to the rain-streaked window, Henry tried to wave a warning. It was difficult for him to tell whether the sudden expression of terror that swept her face was due to seeing him, or the realization that she was in peril.

With a tremendous crack the centuries-old fir tree a few yards from Gladys parted from its appointed place and heeled over toward the raw edge of the cliff. She tumbled down the steepening angle of slippery ground like a limp doll.

The cottage lurched and sagged forward, then paused. Henry gripped the arms of his chair, a veteran sea dog on the bridge of his storm-tossed vessel. As the chair waddled toward the window, he braced his feet against the wall, watching with detached curiosity as Gladys vanished over the crumbling brink, her housecoat a fluttering crimson flag, her hands vainly clawing at the slippery clay. From the kitchen downstairs came the sound of breaking crockery and glassware as the cupboard doors burst open and spewed their contents on the floor which tilted more and more steeply like the deck of a ship in a typhoon.

Henry Morris closed his eyes and waited with a tight little smile.

Eric Cameron's short stories, frequently broadcast on the air, are published in magazines and anthologies in Canada and the USA. His thoughtful, powerful story "Destroying Angel" appeared in our first issue, SSI No. 1.

"Her 'again' had suddenly evoked our parting scene nineteen years ago."

Fine Moon

BY CHI LI

AS I leaned against the ship's railing a crescent-shaped moon rose slowly over the Xiang River. The houses and drooping willows along the riverbanks were bathed in a tranquil, pure light. What a splendid moon.

My feelings, as I gazed, were in turmoil. Nineteen years had added wrinkles to my brow. I related to the poem: "Leaving home when young, now returning old, my local accent has not changed but my hair turns gray."

A small ferry, its wooden oars splashing in the moonlit water, moved slowly across the river. It was the sort of small rowboat I had taken in my childhood when visiting relatives with my mother, but I had not expected to see it again. Not long after, a wooden boat with a patched white sail drifted over. A woman was sitting on her haunches scrubbing the deck and singing in a shrill voice: "He is only two feet tall standing on board..."

I smiled bitterly. The line is from the opera *Child Husband*, and

I was reminded that I myself had been much like a child husband. In those early days, Yuehao, who was three years older and a head taller than me, had chased me around the house every morning to braid my hair.

Yuehao, oh Yuehao, the unlucky woman who had come to my family at the age of five. My parents had adopted her as my sister, but actually she had been my child wife. To make the match more appropriate, they had gritted their teeth and let Yuehao finish primary school. But she still looked the same after she had been educated: her eyes still drooped, her hands tugged at her dress, and her mouth was fixed into a permanent smile. Her response to everything was always, "Yes, Mum." Yuehao followed my mother's instructions and looked after me day after day and year after year. She stopped dressing me only after I started going to high school. After graduating, I entered Fudan University in Shanghai. I departed willingly and for the next nineteen years completely forgot her.

All through college I sacrificed my vacations in order to work for good grades, which meant I did not go home for five years, and when my parents died in 1968, it happened to be at a time in my life when I was both graduating and getting engaged to a Shanghai girl. So even though I was a dutiful son, I still didn't go back home. Later I was assigned to a teaching position in a small remote town in Jiangsu Province. It took us twelve years to get me transferred back to Shanghai, and we exhausted almost all our savings in the process. After that we were busy building a family. It was difficult to find the time and energy to nourish the children emotionally and, given the pressures on the rapidly developing modern Shanghai family in recent years, my wife finally snapped. She picked quarrels constantly and complained in bitter language about the lack of money. I accepted it because I felt it was my fault. I did my best to please her. I tried hard to reawaken her tenderness which I was in desperate need of after so many unsettled years. What joy was there in life if there was no love left between husband and wife? My God, those nineteen years had exhausted me. How could I possibly have had time to think of others? I seldom wrote to my sisters, and as for Yuehao, only my fifth sister had mentioned her in a letter she had written to me after the funeral. She had gone completely out of my mind.

I was only returning because my fifth sister had asked me to sell the old house left by my parents. People still operate on the principle that it is the son's duty to dispose of the property. As soon as she heard about it, my wife nagged me to leave. Without the slightest compunction, she pressed me, as the only son, to appropriate the entire property. My four sisters, on the other hand, wrote proposing that the property be divided equally among the six of us, and I readily agreed. Not long after I had booked my seat on the ship, a letter arrived from my fifth sister, which drew my attention to Yuehao. She asked me not to forget Yuehao and suggested that Yuehao be given a portion of the proceeds. It was then that I learned that Yuehao had married only after she heard I had married the Shanghai girl. After a year, however, her husband had died suddenly and she had been left with two twin boys born after his death. She had lived all this time on a kindergarten teacher's meager salary. Somehow I felt guilty, though I had never promised her anything. I therefore decided to give her some of the money, but I kept this decision to myself. My life was bright in comparison with hers: I live in a big, modern city; I have a television set and washing machine; I have a wife and children and a warm, comfortable home. This thought aroused a rare sense of self-satisfaction in my mind, and I was inclined to be generous.

The ship slowly pulled in to the pier. My heart swelled as I caught sight of Bitao Town, half hidden by the dam and forest. The age-old river, the oars, the sails and songs, Yuehao, and my dear hometown, moved me.

As I looked around the pier, a middle-aged woman approached me and asked softly, "Are you Shangbin?"

"You?" I had recognized the woman but could not believe my eyes. "Yuehao!" I exclaimed.

We stared at each other, numb. Could this be Yuehao? The lovely woman, a head shorter than me, was wearing a well-fitting, neatly ironed dark suit, and her thick hair was combed back into an elegant bun. But I couldn't mistake those bright almond eyes or the mouth curved into a smile. Even the wrinkles and the sagging muscles could not disguise her original self.

"You didn't expect that it would be me who would once again come to meet you," laughed Yuehao, her eyes welling with tears.

For a moment words failed me. Her "again" had suddenly evoked our parting scene nineteen years ago.

"Yes, it's you again. How wonderful!" I changed the subject, trying to avoid reminding her of the sad past. "What about my sisters?"

"They are waiting for you at home. It was too far for them to come. It's evening and they're all old. Do you think you're seventeen again?"

Another "again."

"You have grown," said Yuehao. "You're so tall and strong, with such a heavy beard. The year you left you were still a child. The day the family said good-bye to you..."

"Yuehao, let's stop talking about the past."

Rather than complying with a "Yes, Gou'er," as she had in the past, Yuehao continued. "It's interesting. You are afraid I might feel sad. But how could I? I've never been happier. You've been away for nineteen years. When you left last time, it was also evening and it was the same pier. How could I...All right, all right. Since you don't approve, I'll stop. How are your wife and children?"

Yuehao's openness made me less hesitant.

"Fine, how about yours?"

"They're fine, too." Yuehao replied happily.

The atmosphere became animated. "You've changed a great deal, Yuehao."

"Really?"

"To be honest, when I first saw you, I thought I was on the Nanjing Road in Shanghai."

"Don't make fun of us small-towners. The 'Nanjing Road' of Bitao Town is right around the corner from here. You should see the women in the streets. A lot of them have their hair permed and dress up as smartly as film stars." Yuehao tugged her hair, "I am dressed according to my occupation. A kindergarten teacher's image should be tidy, natural and elegant."

I was both surprised and curious. Her words and movements were full of vitality and had a charming freedom, characteristic of small-town women, which she had lacked during her childhood. Clearly she had learned a lot, and she was much prettier than she had been at the age of eighteen.

The "Nanjing Road" suddenly lay before me, and I couldn't help catching my breath.

A newly-paved asphalt road was lined on both sides with uniquely designed buildings—each one bright and clean. At ground level, shops of all kinds attracted an endless stream of customers, and amid the neon lights many young women were having their hair permed.

"Where are we?" I didn't recognize the place.

"It's Bitao Town," she said deliberately, squinting her eyes to take in the "Nanjing Road."

At the snack stands by the roadside they were selling *Sichuan bean curd*, my childhood favorite. A multitude of emotions stirred within me.

"Well," said Yuehao, "what did you imagine the town would be like? Didn't you see the privately-owned boats touting for business on the side? You should stay a few more days this time, walk the streets, and buy some local products. If you have time, you could come to our kindergarten. We even have pianos there!"

I happily accepted this intriguing proposal.

When we were almost home, Yuehao suddenly became serious. "Shangbin, about the house, would you like my opinion?"

I hastily explained that I had intended to consult all the sisters, including her.

"You don't have to include me," said Yuehao. "My name is Ming Yuehao, not Li Yuehao. We're not related. That's to say, you don't need to include me."

I had no intention of agreeing and told her my plan.

"Yes," interrupted Yuehao. "I appreciate your kindness, but I can't accept your money. If I get money I'm not supposed to, I'll be plagued by my conscience. I know my salary is low, but my sons and I live well. You'll see that when you come to my house. It may even be that I live better than you."

Suddenly my wife's angry face flashed across my mind. "Money, where are we going to get money? Without money, everything is empty."

I looked at Yuehao who was smiling understandingly, her eyes shining with tenderness.

Today was my fourth day back. At lunchtime I received my wife's telegram: "Return immediately after matter settled."

My wife was quite a schemer. Things had finally been concluded yesterday, the six of us each pocketing two hundred yuan, but this time I wasn't prepared to do as she said. Tomorrow was Sunday and I was going to visit Yuehao's family. It was a day I was not going to give up easily.

For several days while dealing with the house, I had thought of Yuehao. The change in her had made me anxious to re-examine my own life to see how much I myself had changed. Yet I hardly dared look. I am middle-aged, I told myself, and mustn't be fanciful. That day I slept until noon. After lunch, I went to the main street and into the first department store, where I bought two "Hero" pens for her sons.

"We even have pianos," I remembered Yuehao saying. Without being aware of it I had arrived at the kindergarten.

A two-story, cream-colored building stood before me. The courtyard, surrounded by a red-brick wall, was divided in two, with a gate separating the playground from the lawn. This explained Yuehao's pride.

Through the railings I saw Yuehao in the distance leading a group of dancing children. A small piano stood nearby, shining in the bright spring sunlight.

I moved closer to get a better view of her.

"Beauty. Beauty. What's beauty?" sang the children.

"Beauty is good manners, politeness and morality," responded Yuehao, who was singing with the children and teaching them to sway their heads and clap to the rhythm of the music. It was the simplest and most childish of dances, yet Yuehao, who had experienced so much of life's pain, could still smile and skip like a child.

A young woman stopped beside me and looked in. "Ah," she smiled. "That's Mrs. Ming, the principal. She's so interesting." "Ming?" I asked. "She's the principal?" "What? You didn't know? She's been in all the newspapers and on the radio because of her advanced teaching methods. She looks just like her picture in the papers. The whole town wants to send their children here. Look, that's my daughter. Since each couple can only have one baby, who wouldn't want the best for it?" "You're right, you're right!" I said, nodding repeatedly. I understood only too well. As a middle school teacher myself I, too, had felt a sense of responsibility and had wanted to cultivate young talent. But life had changed me, and I had busied myself earning a living. The thought of it made me feel the harshness of life. Yuehao, oh Yuehao, I had thought you were a poor small town widow who was probably weak and thin, living a miserable life. How could you have become the opposite of what I had thought? Quietly, I left.

I had supper early, then left for Yuehao's home. It was too long to wait till tomorrow. I needed to confront her now.

"Whom are you looking for, sir?" Yuehao's two sons poked their heads out of the door. Around ten years old, they had the same lovely crescent eyes as their mother.

"I have come to see your mother, Ming Yuehao," I said, noticing they had said "sir" a bit unnaturally. Theirs was probably the first generation of this small town to do so.

They pulled open the door.

"Please come in. Mother hasn't come back yet. She always comes back late. You can sit down if you want to wait," said one boy. "Or, if you're busy, you can leave us a message. Mother discusses everything with us," put in the other.

My goodness! Yuehao had educated her sons to be polite, confident and independent. They were completely unlike my own son and daughter who, spoiled by my wife, told lies at home and were timid everywhere else. I had been deeply concerned about them. Yuehao's two boys, on the other hand, could only be admired. Now I understood the implication of her words, "I have twin sons." At our age our children are our only hope. Yuehao's two rooms were almost empty, except for a few beds and tables. Her poverty was obvious at a glance. Nevertheless, she had two remarkable sons. I couldn't say the same for myself. Oh life, what is it we call happiness?

I was interested to chat with the boys. So I said, "This is not a business visit. I'm a former classmate of your mother's and have come to see her, and her sons. Here's a present for you."

As I pulled the pens from my pocket, their faces turned pink with excitement. They quickly exchanged glances before coming over to express their thanks and tell me their names: the elder one was Jianjian, the younger one Qiangqiang.

We became friends instantly. They were very funny, always speaking together. If one talked loudly, the other talked softly. It seemed they thought identically. I asked to see their exercise books, and they agreed. To my surprise, I found that they had correctly worked out the physics problems posed to ninth grade students, though they were only in the seventh grade.

"You know physics?" cried Qiangqiang. "Are you a teacher? Do you think if we keep this up we will be able to go to Fudan University?"

"Fudan University?" I asked quickly. "Why do you want to go to Fudan University?"

"Mother wishes it. Our uncle studied at Fudan University. Mother said she would be satisfied if we could do as well as him."

"Who is your uncle?"

"Who?" The two boys smiled at each other. "We have never seen him, but Mother often talks about him. Oh, I just remembered, he's back from Shanghai and is coming here tomorrow. You should come too."

"All right, I will. Does your mother tell you any good stories about your uncle?" I asked lightly, reaching out and trying to hide my excitement.

"Boring ones. They are stories about their childhood."

"Are they happy ones?"

"Not always, sometimes...she cries."

My heart sank.

Jianjian was more thoughtful. "It's hard for Mother," he said, gloomily knitting his brow. "She's often lonely. She's OK when she's working, but if she stays at home when she doesn't feel well, we can sometimes hear her secretly crying. We know why, it's because we don't have a father."

I gathered Jianjian into my arms and tried clumsily to comfort him. "Didn't you just say your uncle was coming tomorrow?"

"That's true!" said the two boys perking up again. They told me they were going to send their uncle a very precious gift.

Naturally I pressed them further about this.

"Gold earrings," they said. "Mother has asked us to present them to him."

The gold earrings! So, that's where they had been. I wondered whether Yuehao would have told me about them when she met me if I hadn't stopped her from reminiscing.

On the day I left home, I had been wearing a new indigo-colored suit, my hair had just been done in a crew cut, and I had a new pair of gold earrings. "Put them on your bride's ears when you get married," said my mother, glancing at Yuehao.

The whole family had come with me to the pier. Yuehao helped carry the luggage onto the ship and after she had put everything in order she turned to me. "Gou'er, say something to me."

The ship was about to sail. Dismissing her appeal with a grunt, I merely asked her to remove my earrings and return them to my mother.

"These," she said with tears in her eyes, "Mother says they will protect you from disaster."

"That's a stupid old wives' tale! I'm going to Shanghai. Shanghai! It's a big city. Don't you understand anything?"

Obediently she took off the earrings and, with a sigh, left, her head bent low.

All this time I had thought the earrings were with my sister. Now it appeared that my mother had given them to Yuehao. So that was why she had asked me in her will to marry Yuehao.

I had to leave. I was now more afraid to see Yuehao than ever.

Tomorrow? Why was I staying till tomorrow? Was I going to take the gold earrings back to my wife? The notion was ridiculous!

They belonged to Yuehao, and I would have gladly put them on her ears myself. The thought made my heart pound. Why, at this time of life, had I become so obsessed with a woman, especially the one I had abandoned?

Leave! I pulled myself together and departed.

At six thirty that evening I was queuing up to board the ship. As I waited I periodically looked back, instinctively feeling that Yuehao would come to see me off. I reached the gang plank, but returned to the end of the queue, certain that she would come.

I was the last passenger to board the ship. As it pulled out of the harbor, foghorn blowing, pain stabbed at my heart. I was saying good-bye to my hometown. Suddenly, I seemed to see Yuehao appear on the pier. Her hands reached out to me. In them, I knew, were the gold earrings.

"Gou'er," I seemed to hear her call, "you thought I might feel sad? How could I? I've never been happier."

In a trance, I shook my head, gazing at the empty pier. Yuehao wouldn't come. What a clever woman!

I leaned against the side of the ship and watched my hometown gradually disappear into the distance.

A crescent moon rose above the Xiang River. It seemed to be smiling at me, and soothing me in its rays. I knew I had changed. I was sure I would become invigorated and my life, too, would become rich and exciting. Somehow I would make up for lost time. What a splendid moon over my hometown.

 *Chi Li, born in 1957 in Mianyang, Hubei Province, is an editor of* Fangcao, *a literary magazine in Wuhan. She has written many short stories and novellas and has won a national award for her "Trials and Tribulations." "Fine Moon" brought Chi Li renown when it originally appeared in a collection of works by Chinese women. The story was translated by Wang Ying.*

"I stared at the walls, touched them, rough cold hollow bricks."

Bricks

BY JOSIP NOVAKOVICH

IT is said that physicians are fortunate because their mistakes hide in the ground while their successes bask in the sunshine. Well, with Zivko Zidar and me, the converse is true—the ground hides him as my success.

Zivko came into my office one windy morning, and stood in the doorway, pinching his blue worker's cap in his hands. He was of a medium height, stocky built; his hair was bright gray. "*Herr Doktor*, I would like to talk to you confidentially."

"Shoot."

"Here?"

"Why not? The law and the professional code of honor guarantee that everything you say here, will remain here, strictly confidential."

"But..." He turned his head halfway towards my secretary, whose shirt top was neglectfully unbuttoned, and from his angle, he might see the skin sloping into the brown nipple circle. I smiled.

He looked distraught. He probably didn't trust the feminine ears. I told him to visit me at home after supper, at eight. I was used to the stealthy ways of VD.

"Thank you, thank you. I'm gonna be there." He shook my hand energetically. The skin of his palm was cracked, dry, calloused.

"Don't rush your thanks. With physicians you have to wait until well after the treatment before you thank."

My bell rang at the appointed time, and I was, as usual, alone at home. I used to be married, but my wife had committed suicide—her note, addressed to nobody in particular, claimed that it was because of an affair—a totally insignificant one—I was having with a patient of mine, a nun. My wife had always wanted to be an actress and I think she had failed to diagnose her motive—a bunch of drugged Hollywood actresses had just made suicide fashionable among housewifes.

"Are you alone, *Herr Doktor*?"

"Like a scarecrow. What ails you?"

"I am as healthy as garlic."

"So, how can I help you?"

"I have an unusual request—it calls for a bit of preparation."

Mistrustfully, I watched him as he unbuttoned his fake-fur overcoat and placed it on the armchair shoulders behind him. He leaned—his widow's peak formed a sharp V—and opened a wornout leather bag. I hoped he wasn't pulling a gun.

He took out a bottle of slivovitz. "Here, Doc, *der beste* plum brandy in Slavonia, and *besser* than the Slavonian you can't find. My old man lives to brew his shlivovitza. The Central Committee used to buy it from him."

We downed several shots, grunted to ease the pain in our throats, and chatted aimlessly, it seemed. I got to know that Zivko Zidar had worked as a laborer at Bayer Pharmaceuticals for almost twenty years. That's where he had acquired the habit of sticking German words into his Croatian—he did it far more than I am trying to replicate here in English.

He changed his tone after the fourth shot. "I am tired of working. I *bin zu alt* to start something *neu*. In this life you usually get the second chance, but not the fourth."

"Wait a minute. How old are you?"

"Forty-two. I know I look older and I am older. I have swallowed a lot of dust and worn out many soles."

"But you are a lad! Well, what do you think, how old am I? No need to answer. Sixty-four."

"Doctor, I don't want to kill myself."

"That's not unusual. You need morphine?"

"There's no drug to compare with shlivovitz. What I would like is a certificate that I am dead. Can you make it out for me?"

"What would you do with it? Out of the question!"

"I'd give you a lot of *Geld* for it."

"It's as though you asked me to renounce my profession. No way."

I was convinced that he was out of his mind. I began to think how to get him as far away from me as possible.

"My request won't seem to you so crazy if you lend me your ear for a quarter of an hour."

I walked to the phone. It may be immoral for a physician to unhook his phone; someone in mortal danger could try to call. But, I never know, the phone may be tapped, and my guest could say something political. My elbow brushed a framed picture of me in a military uniform hugging my German shepherd. The picture glass broke to pieces on the floor, and I didn't clean it up. My orange cat sniffed the glass particles. It struck me as stupid that I'd cut off my phone connection with the world, to remain alone with a desperate man.

"The whole thing started early." He talked. "I dropped out of high school because I rushed to make my own money so I could ride motorbikes. I got a job at our barrel factory—on the export line for Bavarian beer—and the work gave me strength during the day and money at night, but it took my future away. I was short-sighted. In youth, your mind is at its peak, and yet, most foolish. But I am not stupid. It's hard to believe..."

"I believe you. But, why do you want a death certificate?"

"I'll get to that. A friend of mine got me a job in Germany, at Bayer. I thought I'd stay for a year, until I bought a good car. Then

I'd go to evening classes, get my high school diploma and enroll at a university to study medicine. I'd wanted to be a doctor, to get into people, into their marrow, the way my nephew does with his toys. Whenever he gets one, he hides in a pigsty and tears it to pieces to see what makes it move. He doesn't have enough patience to dismantle the toy and put it back together. His parents don't buy him toys any more, but I do, just to see him flush with curiosity, and then to see him five minutes later, sullen and sorry.

"*Alles* in *Deutschland* was work. Even walking in the streets was work—signals and signs in a foreign language, rushing bodies, cars. You can't ask for directions because people despise you for not speaking German or English. You start work late and finish it late. After it, you have a couple of beers and fall sleep. The lifestyle got to me, so when I got my first vacation, I thought: This is it. I am not coming back.

"At home I drove around, treated everybody, and met a girl, Miriana. I clung to her as if she could save me from slavery. In Germany, I had no time for whores, let alone honest girls. Where would I have met honest girls?

"Miriana and I made a big wedding. I woke up with a terrible hangover, married, penniless. *Keine Schule* no more. From now on: Push the tool, there's no school. Pull the wheelbarrow, ox, for the new pair of blue sox.

"Her family was like mice in a mouse trap with cheese, except the cheese was gone. Well, we could go back to my old man and be peasants, but you can never go back to the village—our people despise peasants. *Also*, Germany didn't look too *schlimm* from that distance. In a year, we'd spare enough money for an apartment down payment, and then, maybe the Yugoslav economic miracle would start to work.

"I loved Miriana almost as much as myself, but I saw the yoke. I was reined to a cart, my wife sat on it, with a whip and gentle words and tears, and Whip! over my skin, and soon there would be kids there, one on each side, whipping too, so I would pull uphill. Miriana wanted to stay in Brod for a year to finish her last year of high school while I labored *Ausland*. She needed a little room near the school and she needed this and that, all kinds of things, which I sent her from Germany. On *lange Wochenende* I took trains home. I was tired and happy.

"*Aber* the following year I couldn't come back to Yugoslavia for good because of the economic crisis, and she, she wanted to study economics in Zagreb. Every *Dummkopf* studies business or economics, what kind of work will you have? She wouldn't listen. I supported her to become *Damme*. The more I supported her, the more she became a lady, and I the *Arbeiter*.

"Winters in Germany are dark and long, springs and autumns, rainy and *grau*. I dreamed of a house on the Adriatic coast near Zadar. It was expensive to buy a *Hausplatz* but I managed to do it in two years. I kissed the stones where my house would be, and lizards ran out from under them.

"In my free time I drew plans for the house and consulted an architect from Zagreb. He admired my ideas, and we cooperated, but it all cost. Whenever Miriana and I could, we went down to the building site, carried bricks, cleaned around, and then, with cement dust on us, jumped into the turquoise clear water, pulling each other, weightless like cosmonauts.

"In Germany, at night I wondered how she waited for me. Jealousy began to work in me, out of love. But how could it be out of love? Love is trust and jealousy is mistrust. I decided that we needed a child. You need to seal the marriage, give your wife something to do, so she wouldn't start whoring around while I piss blood in the factory. Out of jealousy I thought up my *Lebensplan*. I would step onto the terrace of my villa, wipe my forehead, breathe in the salty air with cypress fragrance, embrace my thankful wife, and listen to my smart son ask me whether there is the end to the sea, and why the water is down and not up, and why the clouds move in the sky and not underground.

"My wife got pregnant. I baked an ox and several piglets and opened up a barrel to piss out a strong stream of brandy for us. It was fall, and fruits were dropping onto cabbage and lettuce everywhere. A hundred people came to the feast, and they ask, 'Who's getting married.' And I tell them, 'My son. He is getting married to mathematics.' 'Where is your son?' 'Here, I point to Miriana's belly.' 'How do you know it won't be a daughter?' 'I know. I'll name him Nadan.' 'But there's no such name—there's only Nenad.' 'Yes, but Nenad means unhoped for, in a good sense, I guess, but my son is hoped for, Nadan.' 'But that's like Nada, a female name for hope,' they say. 'So, can't a man have hope?' I ask.

"And it turned out to be a girl. So much for the power of positive thinking—I read a book on positive thinking, but the stuff doesn't work. *Sehr gut*, I thought. Is there anything more beautiful than a pretty little girl? She'll sit in my lap and I'll tell her fancy tales. I was happy, but the more I looked at her, the stranger she seemed. Even as a baby she is pretty. I am so rough, and neither is Miriana a beauty. We are both blond and blue eyed, and the baby, a dark-eyed brunette. How's that possible?

"I went back to Germany. As I said, whenever there is no trust, there is no love. I imagined all sorts of things—that my wife, behind my back, behind the cliffs of the Alps...she probably wouldn't even know whose the bastard is. No, she isn't a bastard, she's a wonderful baby—too wonderful!

"With such thoughts I ran to the *Bahnhoff* to catch a night train. At *Daemmerung* I break into my wife's apartment, and there she is, sleeping alone, hugging a pillow. I was ashamed. But still I went to the library and read about genetics, and *sicher*, two blue eyed parents can't make *Braune* eyes. I took the case to the court. I won the case, and I lost. As soon as I signed the divorce, I was sorry that I hadn't been *stark* enough to keep my doubts to myself. I understood my lonely wife. People even adopt children. At least one spouse was the real parent—beats adoption by fifty percent. But as soon as I remembered my slave drivers at the factory—all the insults—my eyes turned green.

"I lost my job. I'd left on my jealousy trip without a notice to my boss. I began to drink, and it was a lucky thing that my earnings had been buried in the foundations and walls. Drink and emotion now blurred my mind.

"The aspirin factory took me back after I'd proved that I had gone through a divorce. Divorce is a respectible thing in the West. I wanted to get married again and fill up my house with little screamers. But at a physical examination it turned out my sperm count was too low. So I had relationships. When I had no relationship, I visited whores. Financially, it was all the same—you take out a girl, treat her, and it costs you just as much. Whenever I came, I imagined how many bricks I spurted.

"When you aren't at the *Baustelle*, the construction workers rip you off. They say, 'Why work for a Yugo-Schwabba (a Yugoslav guest-worker in West Germany)—he's got lots, it won't hurt him if we take a sack of cement and a couple of wood planks.' The house slowly got raised to the third floor, a roof was angled over it. But, I still needed *viele Fenster*, plumbing, heating, wiring, marble steps, tiles, mortar, stuccoing, *Farbe*...I couldn't see the light.

"One Christmas I came home. It was cold, windy, and I was forty, and I couldn't find a warm place for my bones. I had put some windows in one room, but they were gone. I stared at the walls, touched them, rough cold hollow bricks. Who am I working for? I ask myself. When I finish, I'll be fifty, done for. Eh, you ox, these walls will bury you. This isn't your home, this is your tomb.

"By the way, isn't it ironic that my last name is *Zidar*? ('mason' in Croatian.) Maybe my name doomed me to get into the wrestling match with the rocks, walls.

"Back in Germany, the thought that the more I worked, the more I buried myself, pricked me like a swarm of wasps. My eyes were swollen. I could barely get up in the morning. I spat blood. Coffee was no help, bitter and upsetting. But, I had to work. What else could I do? Be a bum nobody wants to talk to? But who wants to talk to me anyway? Even if I lived there for a hundred years, no Germans would be my friends. You come out of the *U-Bahn* on the escalator, and stare between the legs of young women in mini-skirts, at the black writing in dripping paint on the yellow walls way up there in the street, AUSLAENDER HERAUS. (Foreigners, get out.)

"You can't fight against your hosts. They exploit you, but that's all right. I like exploitation—it means there's a salary, somebody thinks you are useful. To Germans lately you seem something smuggled in, a tool that's outgrown its use. Everywhere you have to watch your step, and work according to St. Mark's Gospel. In the Bible they don't give you Mark's last name, and there they do. Deutsch. St. Deutschmark.

"By the way, Doctor, do you know that joke about Germans and Yugoslavs?"

"Which one?"

"Just imagine how it would be if the Germans had won the Second World War. *Ja*, we would be forced to work in Germany, while they sunbathed at the Adriatic coast."

"That's just what has happened. Anyway, I did finally decide to come back to Yugoslavia for good. The Yugoslavia I had left twenty years before doesn't exist any more. Old hospitality, kindness, talkativeness, generosity, that's all gone. Around Zadar people hate me as a usurper, Yugo-Schwabba, a Serb, though I am not, so where do I belong? You don't notice these things if you stay for a weekend, but after staying for months, you suffer. I watch my big house and say, 'Eh, my grave, where is my name? How many years before you take me in?' And the idea suddenly pops up, If my house is my gravestone, let me make a gravestone.

"I rushed to Germany, and was rehired. My life got a new meaning: My Tomb. I would sell the house and build a mausoleum. I was no longer in a hurry. I realized the Germans were *wirklich gemuetlich* and kind. My German became smooth, my grammar good. Nobody insulted me—the wisdom of the grave shone out of me.

"Every morning I woke up before sunrise and whistled with the blue sparrows at the open window. I was rejuvenated. Everything was now so good that I suspected I could still start from scratch. Even my sperm count might go up if I ate enough caviar. But I knew better. I loved the things around me only because I had hated them. I was free from them, I could leave any moment, I was leaving. Closing my *Augen*, I could see my destination, HEREIN LIES IN PEACE ZIVKO ZIDAR.

I continued to *arbeit* for a couple of years. I got a promotion; became a supervisor. I sold my house and bought a *Platz* on the edge of the Slavonski Brod cemetery. My old man's house would be thirty meters away from the tomb, over the railroad tracks, Munich to Athens. I kneeled to kiss the soil and the ants that walked it. I dreamed the plans for my tomb. I saw the tomb from the above, below, inside, outside. The walls shifted in my mind, changed shapes, stretched out, rose, slid into the ground, they combined into pyramids, towers rising and sinking, and finally, the idea of sinking took over. I settled the tomb below the *Grund*, at least twenty meters deep, with a cap above. It would be energy efficient: in the summer, cool, in the winter, warm.

"I've made indents in the tomb-floor to fit positions of my body, like an embryo, like a dead man on the back, like an elbowing Roman eating grapes, reclining like a dental patient, kneeling with a support for my belly like a drowned swimmer. I have a library there—religion, history, philosophy—and a *Grundig* stereo system with thousands of religious music tapes. In my afterlife, I will have *genug Zeit* to think, and..."

I couldn't keep my attention throughout. His plans reminded me how as a boy I had visited my grandfather in his village one summer. Grandmother, Father, an uncle and two aunts showed me Grandfather in an open casket in the dark, with candles on the four corners, white powder on Grandfather's gray face, and told me he had died of too much drink. Then they carried him out in the casket and put him in a hole underground, sang chants, wept, gave speeches. They had all worn black. Father axed the bottom of a varnished cross into a sharp spear, and stuck it into the mound on the grave, amid bunches of flowers. I hadn't known that Grandfather had built a fallout shelter with a large supply of cans. I'd wept for him for two days, and on the third, as I'd been twisting chicken necks backwards to see how death works, he staggered out of the tomb, his chin stubbly, and I believed he'd been raised from the dead. He then read to me about Biblical resurrections. For a whole year I'd been the greatest believer around, reading nothing but the Bible, praying hours on end on my knees. But the following summer there was no cross and my grandfather had left the shelter open. I'd walked in, saw the opened and rusted cans, and decided nobody would ever again make a fool out of me.

Now I laughed to myself at the memory.

"You may laugh," Zivko said, "but I'm on the right path."

"And on what grounds do you believe there's an afterlife?" I asked.

"There is too much suffering here that there shouldn't be a

better life afterwards."

"That's like saying that because my rotten tooth gives me too much pain, once it falls out, a better one will grow in its place which will give me pleasure!"

"But we do go through two sets of teeth. Why not two lives?"

"The second set is more painful. By that analogy, if there is afterlife, there's only hell and no heaven."

"Oh, you simply don't remember the childhood pains. The first set probably hurt more."

"So, when you die, you think another you will grow, like the second tooth, but in whose mouth? In the mouth of God? And what will God bite with you as his tooth?"

Zivko laughed and two silver teeth, dead teeth, faced me like little tombs.

"We always hope and we are always disappointed. We think we hope for something that could be found here, but *wirklich* we hope for something deeper. We feel there's something better. Afterlife."

"You feel it. How can a feeling be that informative? Hot? Cold? Tingling? Tart? Feelings are sensations, not thoughts, not information about something far out, but about something right here, something that touches your tastebuds, your skin, your retina, your eardrum. Feelings don't answer metaphysical questions."

He looked at me with pity as if I were sick and there was no cure for me. "You are a physician; of course you're gonna think physical. But, you see, the Bible too tells there's *Leben* after *Tod.*"

"The Bible says all sorts of things. How about this, 'I said in mine heart concerning the estate of the sons of men, that God might manifest them, and that they might see that they themselves are beasts. For that which befalleth the sons of men befalleth beasts; even one thing befalleth them: as the one dieth, so dieth the other; yea, they have all one breath; so that a man hath no preeminence above a beast: for all is vanity.' *Ecclesiastes.* See?"

It took him awhile to digest that, along with another shot of plum brandy, which rallied his spirits. "On the German TV I saw *Life after Life.* People float when they..."

"Spare me that hallucinogenic bullshit. When you are falling asleep, you hallucinate. Of course you are going to hallucinate when you are dying; death is a tempestuous biochemical event. Your center for balance is affected, your inner clock misfires..."

I was about to punch on, but he looked groggy, his head in his palms, his creases rising even into the smooth bays aside his silverized widow's peak. He looked like a poor Jack Nicholson, without enough money to dye his hair, if such a picture could be imagined. We kept silent for several long minutes, long as if the conversation had died, and the death of it changed our time perception. The minutes seemed like hours, and I was reminded how a thousand years is like one day, and one day like a thousand years to God.

He broke the silence. "Doctor, yes, you did hit a sore spot. Yes, I don't know that there is life after death. Yes. That is why I am here. I need preparation. Give me a *Zertifikat* so I could go my way, get myself and everybody else used to the idea of my death. And I'll be waiting for the eternity."

"Why not among the people?"

"You die alone. Groups can't teach you nothing about death. If there's *Leben* In *Ewigkeit*, I don't want to meet it in a decrepit body, locked in a coffin."

"You are naïve. Bodies rot fast."

"Damn you, you aren't gonna spoil my plan." He stood up and hovered above me, waving his big arms in rage. "I need my space! Give me my papers!"

"It's not that simple. Anyway, what are you after—a life insurance scam?"

"Don't you tell me it's not simple. You know that our people die like mice, and nobody questions any deaths. One relative and one doctor, or just one doctor is enough to certify."

"I am afraid you are right."

"How much?"

"It'll be on the house. Well, give me a dozen liters of that plum brandy."

"Don't be that cheap. I could sign you up for one third of my life insurance policy."

"I knew it." I threw up my arms in despair. Once a Yugoslav, always a crook.

"I'll give you one half, three hundred thousand Deutschmarks spread over fifteen years, if you promise that you'll ship me the newest findings in parapsychology, the newest medical findings on the soul, the newest religious thinking. I'll show you the slot."

"A doctor can't get his patient's life insurance. That's absurd. I'll be jailed."

"Doc, don't be naïve. Who's gonna worry? The cops? They are too busy stealing. The Germans? They are too regular, it beats their imagination."

"And what about your father?"

"He'll testify that I am dead even if my chest moves like a chest of a dead actor in a movie. He wants to get there too. When I am abroad, he hangs around in my tomb and when I come home, he pretends to live in his little house, doing yard work, chopping the wood. In the tomb I find his white hairs caught in the radio antenna, the dial's shifted to the folksongs channel, the place reeks tobacco and brandy, his footprints are on the Iraqi carpet. But once I get there, I'll lock up the tomb, I'll never get out, and he'll join me only when he's dead, in a separate little room. Doctor, there's space even for you there, one stylish room, medium size, with sauna. I kind of like you. What do you say?"

It was late, the old clock in my corridor banged eleven, a brassy, yellow sound. We agreed upon the time and place.

As planned, I scribbled out a certificate once I got to his father's home a week later. His father ran out screaming for the priest in his broken voice while I injected a sleeping drug into Zivko's buttocks. The priest walked around the body, swinging his cup of incense, sang below the key, crossed himself, spat his phlegm into the pail of ashes next to the stove, all routine. The old man and I placed Zivko in the coffin we had bought at the neighborhood undertaker's, and the mortician showed up only to nail the lid. He was so drunk that he missed the nails several times, and crushed his thumbnail, screaming like a whipped child. So, I myself nailed Zivko in. Of course, I hadn't forgot to enclose in the coffin a hammer, chisel, pliers—small tools a mason should need.

The procession was medium: a local brass band, senior citizens, a priest, nuns, school comrades. Four men lowered the coffin into the tomb on two rasping ropes, and let the heavy stone fall over the entrance with a bang which resounded and echoed deep in the ground for a long time, shaking us all above.

Now and then on my evening walks with my mongrel dog, I stop by the heavy tomb and light a candle. The tomb looks like an abstract partisan monument, the type that was in fashion twenty years ago, with black marble wings, pentagonal, smooth, reflecting moonlight. ZIVKO ZIDAR is grooved, with 16.X.1948 for his birthday, 23.X.1990 for his deathday. His color picture, inlaid in stone, egg-shaped, gold-rimmed, gives me his startled stare, from above his thin moustache and pursed lips in ambitious self-denial. My dog growls at the picture, tears away the leash out of my hands and runs home. The insides of the letters away from the main inscription gleam out quotes of wisdom in Latin, Cyrillic, Greek, Hebrew, German Gothic—a script each side of the pentagon. Two pots sit below his name like trophies, and sometimes I place white tulips there, but most often a slice of roasted mutton with crackling skin, something for the owls.

I walk back on the path through the freezing mud, scrape my muddy soles over the gravel and the stainless steel of the rails, and I go on to his father's moss-covered mud house. Late in the evening the lights are out. I sneak into the backyard, a dog yawns and comes out of a bread-baking brick oven, and he doesn't bark. He smells my shoes and yawns even wider in loneliness. I tug at his hanging ears, promising I'd bring along my mutt next time. I open a lid inside the brick oven and insert the *New England Journal of Medicine*, *Deutsche Wissenchaft*, and the *Ecumenical ESP Quarterly*, and listen to how the journals slide.

Above an empty chicken coop, with years-old frozen chicken shit trapping pigeon feathers on the splintery wood, I check the electric meter. Two wires branch off from the house towards the mausoleum, sinking. The meter disk rotates swiftly with a little hiss. The red stretch comes back every second, and I know that the student of death still clings to life, trying to cheat death on the border of the cemetery, beneath the cemetery.

Born in 1956, in Daruvar, Slavonia, Yugoslavia (now Croatia), Josip Novakovich writes short stories in his native Croatian and in English, and on occasion translates stories by his fellow countrymen into English. His stories have appeared in several publications in Croatia and neighboring countries, as well as in American publications. He is presently in the USA.

"Who does not have eccentricities and whims?"

The Bath

BY PANOS IOANNIDES

SHE adjusted her spectacles and looked at him. With the sponge, which perspired fragrant bathsalts, he was now rubbing his thighs and knees. She consulted her watch again. Another hour yet: half for his calves, half for his feet. His shadow on the wall reminded her of a locust. She took off her glasses for presbyopia, put on those for myopia and bent over the horoscope again.

"Lucky number four. Lucky color yellow. Emotional calm."

What was his name? Six or seven? Cri-, three; -ton, six. Of course! Two more than Noni.

"Lucky number five. Lucky color..."

"After your bath I'll make you a hot cup of tea to help you sleep," she told him. "Should I bring you your blue nightclothes?"

"Yesterday's," he replied and regarded her severely through his glasses, which he insisted on wearing even in the bath. They were misted with condensation. "Give me the towel."

She wiped them five times on her yellow robe.

"Mona phoned. She'll drop by to see us," she told him.

"What does she want?"

"She'll bring the clock."

"I hope he doesn't come too..."

"I shouldn't think so. He works in the afternoons."

"What time is it?"

"Three and a quarter hours exactly!"

"I asked the time."

"Twelve!"

She returned to her newspaper. She still had forty-five minutes at her disposal. He would not leave the bath before his four hours were up. Four and a quarter hours in the morning. Four hours in the afternoon. For a year now he had not deviated from the schedule even once. When Noni had asked him in admiration how he managed to be so exact without a watch, he had regarded her ironically and said something which disconcerted her:

"Are you sure you are not daydreaming?"

But of course she was sure! For months now she had been his shadow. From the very first day she had noticed that he stayed shut in the bathroom longer than normal; it was the day of Mona's wedding, she had suspected that something serious was happening. She began watching him secretly, trying to find out what was going on. At first out of fear, in case he was ill. Later, when she was sure that it was nothing more than a new habit, to help him. Now she knew the process in every detail. Moreover, he himself asked her to stay with him recently.

The reasons, however, for his strange behavior remained unknown to her. She could not bring herself to ask him directly, all she could do was prove to him that he was clean. This she attempted repeatedly and discreetly, but without success. Neither her "spontaneous" compliments about his cleanliness, nor the mirrors she carefully placed opposite his favorite armchairs, succeeded in convincing him. The only thing she ventured to do was to consult, first, his niece. "You are the only person who understands my uncle!" she replied. And then her stepson. "I could never understand Father." He did, however, provide a plausible explanation for the marathon of cleanliness: "I see Father still keeps office hours!"

Perhaps that was it! The eight and a quarter hours in the bath corresponded with the timetable he had pedantically followed for years. But Noni hoped that was not the explanation, that it was simply a coincidence. She remembered that after the marriage of her stepson, her husband, in spite of the fact that he was over seventy-five, had doubled his working hours. Shortly before his doctor had compelled him to retire he had been working sixteen to eighteen hours a day. If the two, consciously or not, had indeed become identified in his mind, there was a danger that...

"And what do you do when you want to use the bathroom?" asked their daughter-in-law cheerfully.

"I wait until your father has finished," replied Noni.

It was the first time since she had joined the family that their daughter-in-law had shown an interest in their problems; she insisted on learning more details. But Noni changed the subject. It was not right to discuss such things with others. It was better to keep them to herself. Only she would be able to understand if he ever decided to give her an explanation, no one else! She was the only one who knew that those hours in the bath were unwarranted! But in whom could she confide and admit it was that, especially, which comforted her. Who would believe they were not really necessary at his age? Who would not be eager to connect them with all his other eccentricities? Of course, she had to admit that in the past his eccentricities had been innocent and less annoying for others. Simply habits. He could not tolerate the smell of cheese, for example. (Now he was allergic to all milk products.) Or, he could not bear a stranger to be in the room when he was eating. (Now he could not bear the maid in the house after the morning bath.) As regards food, sleep and lovemaking, he was always a creature of habit. The orderliness, then, which characterized every habit he cultivated now, after his enforced retirement from the business, was only natural. That of the bath was the second. The first was the "pips and the crumbs." In a silver cup he saved all kinds of pips. "Fuel for the fireplace" and the crumbs, "for the sparrows!" At first he confined himself to his own crumbs and his own pips. Later he imposed the habits on her. But

Noni forgave him. In serious matters he showed understanding. He never humiliated her as so many of his class do when they marry poor girls. Nor did he show that he harbored any resentment that she had not presented him with a child, in spite of the fact that she suspected that that was the only reason he had married her after the death of his first wife. Of course, he had never tolerated Mona; "perhaps because she is the only relative of yours I get on with," she had once complained to him. "And the only one who has remained faithful to us to the point of self-sacrifice!" "She doesn't do it as disinterestedly as you imagine," he answered her. "The hoyden can't wait for me to be gone."

But even so, this certainly did not prevent him from providing a generous dowry for the daughter of his sister. And he continued to help her in spite of the fact that the girl failed to realize that he did so more willingly when he did not see too often in his house "those sly eyes that pretend they do not want anything..."

He especially disliked Mona's husband. The first time he saw him, "I was afraid to touch him," he admitted to her. "You think you are touching mucus..." She disagreed. Polys was polite and helpful. He was not the ideal son-in-law they could have found, but he was not the worst. He had a secure little position and the realization that he was marrying a girl who was socially superior to him; facts that ensured he would respect his marriage vows.

She liked Polys for another reason, too, which she could not admit to, of course. For the understanding he showed for her passion for horoscopes and palmistry. He supplied her with every publication which had even a single column about astrology. At first she had hidden them and read them when she was alone. Now, with the new situation, she could not occupy herself with her hobby, unfortunately, except during the hours that Criton was asleep.

"The other one didn't phone?" The old man asked, interrupting her thoughts.

"No, dear."

She saw his scrawny body emerge from the steam. She got up and gave him the bathrobe.

He could not forgive the indifference of his son and daughter-in-law. Recently their visits had become more infrequent.

"Their work, the children, their obligations," Noni made excuses for them. "Satiation," he said. "They got their hands on the old man's money, why should they bother him any more?" This indifference of his son made him regard the frequent visits of his niece as provocation. He was convinced that she and her husband went to the trouble with just one aim: to show him who really loved him and who he ought to remember when the time came. They did not know, nor would they find out as long as he lived, the surprise he had in store for them.

Noni helped him put on his underwear and his blue pajamas. Then she combed his hair and threw a few drops of perfume in his hands.

"I hadn't completely finished, but I can't stand to feel you waiting for me."

"But I..."

"I know you," he interrupted her in the middle of her protest.

They went into the living room. He sat in the overstuffed armchair and stretched out his hand towards her. She put on his watch.

"Exactly on time," she told him.

He checked the watch against the two wall clocks, with the pendulum clock in the hall and the three table clocks, whose metallic voices refreshed the room. They were all perfectly synchronized.

He sank into his chair, half-closed his eyes and began following the hands of the clocks. It was his favorite occupation after having his bath. And his second serious habit which had developed into a biological need. In fact recently his life had become divided between these two *needs*, as he himself called them: to rid himself of dirt and to know the exact time at every moment. When the children had been in the habit of coming and seeing them he had had a third *need*, the telephone. He would call them every day and give them advice by the hour about this and that, from which investments were most secure to what was the best way of doing their shopping, or he would ask for information about business and about political developments. However, since the day that his daughter-in-law's maid and his son's secretary, as though by agreement, had begun to make excuses not to call them to the phone, it began to cause him migraine and he ordered it to be removed to the hall.

It was about that time that the water heater had broken down. As he was waiting for the water to heat up on the gas he suddenly found it difficult to breathe, he complained that the dirt was entering his pores, his eyes, his ears, descending his gullet. He began to grunt, to gesticulate like a man who was drowning. Noni was compelled to undress him and sit him in the bath. For four hours she poured over him warm water which she brought from the kitchen and to scrub him, because he himself was exhausted. She fell ill after that. On the first day he prepared her breakfast and was tender. So much so that she plucked up the courage to ask him for the first time what was the matter with him, why he thought he needed to take such a prolonged bath.

"You'll be telling me I'm mad next," he rebuked her. "Instead of taking care to clean the house a little, you complain about me. Wherever you touch in here you get dirty. How do you manage to bring so much dirt in? Is it you who brings it or is your protegé?"

And she did not see him again until the day she was better and emerged from her room.

If they had a child, someone to look after her...If she could have persuaded Mona to come and live with them. Now that she was married it was no longer possible. And she would have been even more afraid of her uncle. She had always been afraid of him. All the time she had lived with them, the unfortunate girl, she had tried to remain invisible. She went about on tiptoe, she made sure her uncle was asleep before going into the bathroom, that he was in his study at the other end of the hall before opening the refrigerator. At table she scraped her plate with lowered eyes and strove to anticipate his every wish. And when he gave her pocket money she would blush furiously, unable to find the words to thank him.

She was an orphan and they were her only relatives. If they had not taken her in after the death of her parents, God knows what would have become of her!

Yes, he was a good man, they should not complain. Who does not have eccentricities and whims? Especially at such an age, after such an Odyssey! From the Reformatory to the Summit!

The sound of conversation awoke him. He opened his eyes. He was in the armchair still, covered by a blue blanket. Between his legs, wrapped in a piece of worn yellow cloth, the hot water bottle rested.

Noni and his niece were sitting near the window, laughing softly. Before them were arrayed cups, the remains of a sweet, some savories. Noni's face was flushed with the emotion that only dabbling in the mystery of her fate could arouse! Her eyes shone with an insatiable curiosity. The girl was paler and more transparent than she had been when she had lived with them. In other respects she did not seem to have changed. He just found her a little plumper. It was understandable. With all the deprivations which that colorless husband must have imposed on her...

He got up and silently went and stood behind them. He glanced at the newspaper. It was old. At least two months. He might have known it. The horoscope in that issue was favorable, it was one of the few cases in which it was favorable for both of them in the same edition.

He bent and seized the newspaper...

"Did you wake up?" exclaimed Noni, and she began to tidy up the tea service which she had knocked over when she was startled.

"Forgive us, Uncle. We woke you up."

"Very late," he said, and returned to his armchair with the newspaper.

He screwed it up and threw it in the fireplace, watching carefully the expression on Noni's face. He was impressed by her composure. He saw her lower her gaze and laugh softly.

"It was an old one," she told him.

However much he tried he could not detect any trace of irony in her voice. Just a certain playfulness.

"I brought your clock," Mona said. "It was a small fault."

"Put it there and give me the receipt."

The girl replied that she did not get a receipt, "it was too small a sum to mention."

"I asked how much it cost," the old man insisted.

"Five shillings."

"Noni, I have some change in the drawer of my desk."

Noni get up obediently. He began to pace the room, leaning on his stick. He did not look at the girl. Now and then he stopped and listened to one of the clocks. Only the Swiss cuckoo clock needed winding up. He did it carefully.

In the detecting of every anomaly in his clocks he was infallible. His cold white fingers, when he rested them on one, became more sensitive than a cardiologist's stethoscope. His ear registered the most insignificant peculiarity in its pulsation. And he could never accept failure, neither in the timely diagnosis of any small malfunction, nor in its cure. They had to work irreproachably, obediently, to be preserved and maintained, to fill the grandeur of every minute they conquered with their polyphonic rhythm. When the gold-inlaid Florentine clock, which now shone with health, had suddenly stopped, he had panicked. He collapsed in a chair and everything around him went dark. He felt a strong constriction of his heart, and neither the ether which Noni sprinkled on him, nor the massage by the soft, disgusting hand of Polys, brought him round. He was not even angered by that contact. And that worried him even more, he just asked to see his son. The young man went and telephoned. Unfortunately they were away on a trip. While he...Then, from within the haze he heard Mona's husband say something original and witty:

"...impossible I tell you! He's suffered apparent death..."

That watery voice, those two broken, choked phrases, filled him with optimism. He gave in to the fatigue and slept. In vain they called the doctor. He had not died, of course he heard them in his sleep. And it did not matter that he could not interrupt them, to tell them that the words "apparent death" were the key, that although they had been spoken about him, they were absolutely correct for the Florentine clock.

Two days later, when he came to, his first thought was to send it to be repaired.

He went to the table and began to caress it. He lifted it to his ear. On its surface was still a trace of perspiration from the girl's hand, and a small spot of oil. The bronze gave off an intense foreign smell. He started to clean it insistently, while a fine gossamer stream of mud, vaporous as usual at first, began to flow from the nape of his neck down his backbone. The spot of oil, despite all his attempts to remove it from his hand, to which it had been transferred as soon as he touched it, stuck and spread all over his fingers, and millimeter by millimeter conquered his palm.

He turned and regarded the girl. She smiled at him.

"Why don't you wash?" he asked her "Is that tramp of a husband of yours miserly with the water, too?"

She looked at him, offended.

"Why do you say that, Uncle?"

He took a step back, displeased by a smell given off by her body and which he could not identify. The stream of mud on his back branched into tributaries, some descending to his thighs, one climbing the hairs of his abdomen, one slowly entering the large intestine.

"You smell," he told her, and sank into his chair. The movement caused the mud to spread to large areas on his body, sticking the material to his flesh.

"Uncle..."

"Stop calling me Uncle. I am not your uncle. Tell me, have you made love with that rabbit?"

"I don't recognize you," said the girl, and got up.

"Don't answer me back, you fat animal. You are soiled by that person and you come here satiated and foul-smelling to pass comments to me."

"I'm sorry, Uncle, if you really feel like that about me," Mona replied and ran outside.

In the corridor she met her aunt. The old man heard hurried, choked words and tears and angrily slammed the door. The impudent wretches who think they can ransom a will with five shillings. He had disinherited all of them, his son too, even Noni. For long enough they had benefited from his toil and sacrifices, the fruits of his life, which had sprouted in rubbish and poverty to ripen in omnipotence. "Of a life crowned with vindication!" the Minister had said at the gathering organized in honor of Criton by the Association of Pharmaceutical Suppliers. He, unfortunately, had been unable to attend, it was the time of his bath, but he had been informed of the proceedings by a colleague, who had visited him on the very same evening. They had called him a pioneer, who in three decades had suceeded in making the supply of pharmaceuticals an autocracy, in increasing prices a hundredfold, in so inspiring the enterprises that the local market followed hard on the heels of scientific developments, something that was only feasible in advanced countries! He was also informed of the sensation created by his suggestion, which was conveyed to the assembly by his son, that an end should be demanded in a dynamic way to the unlawful competition with the class of pharmaceutical suppliers by the State. Through the free provision of drugs to the poor, the Government was putting at risk a flourishing private enterprise. His suggestion was that such items should certainly be supplied by the Government pharmacies, but for payment, with a discount of twenty percent on current prices and only on presentation of a checked certification of poverty.

It was approved unanimously. Also unanimously the same gathering proclaimed him lifetime President of the Association, and the Minister, with commendable modesty, declared that "men of such many-sided and multifarious talents ought to occupy the highest Ministerial offices in the Government."

The toast proposed by the Secretary of the Association was clever too: "Let us drink to the health of the eminent man who managed to earn such an income that he could easily have been taxed at twenty-one shilling to the pound if he had not had me as chief accountant!"

Something dripped on him from the chandelier. He ran his fingers through his hair and shook it off. It was a sticky substance. It smelled like wet camphor, no, like penicillin with orange essence. He tried to get rid of it with his other hand, but ended up dirtying that one too. He found it hard to unstick one hand from the other. He moved away from the chandelier. With the movement he felt the mud creep on his thighs. He lowered his blue pajama trousers and threw them in the corner. That revolting earthy smell! No, he did not regret his decision to leave his property to the firm in Leipzig, the famous firm of crematorium manufacturers. In return they would undertake to establish crematoria in all the towns of the island. Everyone who hated the damp and the micro-organisms of the earth would be taken care of free of charge in memory of the donor. As for himself, his will was explicit. They would embalm him and send him without escort, that was a condition, to Leipzig. "Per necessaria..."

He took off his dressing gown, his pajama jacket and his vest. Then, with an effort, his underpants.

He looked at the clock. It was less than an hour since he had got out of the bath. The water would not yet have heated up. He ought to wait for a long time yet. He stood motionless in the middle of the room with his eyes fixed on the pendulum which continued to trace its perfect arcs. Every time the well-polished bronze cut the pale outline of his shadow it became flaccid, dark, and its metallic flesh was covered with blisters and bulges which resembled the craters of the moon.

The door opened. Noni came in. She was so confused that she certainly did not notice that he was naked, nor that as she approached him she dragged his underclothes and pajamas with her slippers.

"I'll never forgive you for that," she told him. "You are evil! You blame others and quarrel with those who love us, who have remained faithful to us. Have you forgotten what she has done for us, that unhappy girl? How many sleepless nights, what trouble, what care? Who else would have done it? Who else would have stayed here for so many years to look after you, to wash you, to change you, to touch you? The other one? Who never gave you more than the tip of her finger? You never dared quarrel with them, though, when you would have been justified. Because you know that they don't need us. That they don't care what happens to us. Do you know why the girl came here? She is expecting a child. She came to tell us first, before she tells her husband. Us! And you threw her out. You made her cry. I tell you, I've had enough. Enough. I can't stay here any longer. Not another moment. I, who with calling you 'my love' for so many years used to forget your name and look secretly at your passport and our marriage certificate to remember it. Stay with your clocks and your fears, which you need more than you need me...Why did you do this to me? Because you know how much I love her?"

He could not hear her any more. He had set off with slow steps for the bathroom. He entered and quietly closed the door. He locked it. He heard her speaking, as though he was still before her, as though she had not noticed that he had left. Then her voice faded away in the depths of the house.

He took off his slippers and went to the bath. Under the slimy layer of mud and the smell of penicillin he felt his skin smart. He sat on the small stool. A chill pierced him. He turned the tap on. The water was icy. His members under the mud began to receive the cataract. He crouched, holding his knees, and let the water stab him.

Sometimes cold water warms more. Perhaps it cleans better too. He felt something hard under his chin. It was his watch. He removed it and placed it carefully on the hard sponge, which for the first time did not crawl, hungry for mud, over his body.

The seconds surrounded him mercilessly...

He was brought to by muffled bangings. No they were not demolishing the house, as he had imagined, it was banging on a door and a distant voice. An old voice, it seemed to him...

"Open up, you crazy old man. Why did you lock the door?"

He did not reply. He turned the cold water tap fully on, at the same time turning off the hot water tap, which was not hot. For the first time he discovered that he could tolerate cold water, that the first few seconds only were difficult.

The voice outside was insistent:

"Criton! Criton!"

He could only just hear her. Then the shouts faded and stopped altogether.

When the four hours were up he rose. Holding the shower pipe he stepped out of the bath and headed for the door. He dragged himself along the corridor holding on to the wall. His whole body burned and he felt his eyes wedged deeper and deeper into their sockets, like two cold, frozen, pebbles. Only his eyes still preserved the chill of the water.

He opened the door. He shuffled in, leaving rivulets on the carpet and fingerprints on the furniture and on the clocks, which restrained him and supported him with a polyphonic ticking which all the time became stronger, louder.

In his large, overstuffed armchair, opposite his favorite mirror, Noni was sprawled. Beside her was a suitcase, hastily packed, from whose frayed mouth protruded some of her beloved floral dresses.

Noni was sleeping with her glasses for myopia perched crookedly on her nose and her nostrils full of mucus which she had not had time to wipe away before she had fallen asleep.

Straddling the Florentine clock, upside down, her glasses for presbyopia shone.

He quietly opened her suitcase and selected a yellow dress with which he wiped her nose. Then, with an effort, he picked up his blue bathrope and threw it over her knees.

He stood there, numb and naked, in front of her for a moment and then went into the kitchen to prepare her a hot water bottle.

Born in 1935, in Famagusta, Cyprus, Panos Ioannides studied in Cyprus, the United States and Canada, He started his career as a journalist. In 1955 he was appointed Program Officer at Cyprus Radio. Since then he has held a number of senior posts both in radio and television. At present he is Head of TV Programs at the Cyprus Broadcasting Corporation. Mr. Ioannides writes poetry, plays, short stories, novels, numerous scripts for radio, and serials, plays and documentary scenarios for television. He has been awarded four National Prizes for Prose in Cyprus. His play Gregory won first prize at the Fifth International Festival of TV Plays held in Sofia, Bulgaria, in 1976; his play Onisilus was awarded first prize by the Society of Cypriot Playwrights in 1980. He is President of the Cyprus PEN Club. His translator, David Bailey, was born in England, in 1947. Mr. Bailey lived in Cyprus since 1970 where he worked as a broadcaster and news editor for the Cyprus Broadcasting Corporation, and as a freelance translator. He has recently settled in France. Mr. Ioannides' story "Gregory" appeared in SSI No. 62.

"All this talk about earthquake-proof buildings is rubbish."

Complete Destruction, Absolute Disaster

BY JOHN HAYLOCK

IT was a mistake to mention the recent earth tremor that slightly shook Tokyo, alarmed me, but caused no casualties or serious damage. In Tokyo, the possibility of an earthquake often creeps into a conversation. I was lunching with Vincent, an old Tokyo friend (we once taught at the same university), at the coffee shop of a large hotel.

Since retiring from Japanese academic life, I have been unable to resist visiting Tokyo every autumn. There is something about the capital of Japan that is very beguiling. The city is a mess and a muddle, the crowds are oppressive, the public transport groans under the weight of the thousands of passengers each train has to carry. Traveling in the subway is more like a punishment than a pleasure: the crush is almost rib-breaking, often button removing, and one can land on a platform with only one shoe. And yet...the place is stimulating. Is it the activity, the frenzy all around one, or is it the sort of sensuality that pervades the air that makes it so?

Whatever it is, I am inexorably drawn back to Tokyo every year and I enjoy my stay.

"Did you notice the tremor the other day?" I asked Vincent. He and I were drinking gins and tonic at our table in the restaurant prior to beginning lunch.

When Vincent downed the rest of his second gin and tonic and glared at me through his bushy, beetling eyebrows, I knew I was in for one of his portentous statements. "You know what's going to happen, don't you?"

"No."

"Complete destruction. Absolute disaster."

"Of what?"

"Of this city, of course," he said, irritably. "Millions dead. Millions"

"You mean an earthquake? *The* earthquake people keep prophesying?"

Vincent's eyes blazed. "The slight tremor we had the other day was nothing, nothing."

"It alarmed me."

"It alarmed everyone because each time there is a tremor, people wonder if it is *it*."

"It?"

"The real thing. You know there hasn't been an earthquake, a big one, since 1923, and from all prognostications, calculated pronostications by experts, one is due at any moment. Tokyo lies on top of a fault. The fracture in the sub-crust has to move. It must do so. These tremors happen all the time. Most of them can't be felt, but the seismographs register them."

"But won't the little tremors relieve the tension, make the sub-crust settle down a bit?"

A waiter served us with our soles bonne femme and glasses of white wine; there seemed to be more mashed potato and béchamel sauce than fish. Vincent looked at his plate and lit a cigarette. "It's all a matter of the sub-strata being unstable." He put the tip of his cigarette between his teeth and held out his rather shaky hands and moved them up and down. "Something's got to give. It was sheer madness to have the capital in Tokyo. To build it right over a geological fissure."

"The shoguns lasted nearly three hundred years here."

Vincent put out his cigaratte, forked up a little of his fish and potato and took a sip of wine. "There's a Japanese professor, a distinguished seismologist, who says—do you know what he says and he knows what he is talking about?"

"No. What does he say?"

Vincent dilated his eyes. "He says that the whole city should be moved at once."

"But that's impossible. There are about thirty million in the whole area if Kawasaki and Yokohama and so on are included."

"The Emperor and the government offices anyway should leave."

"But where could they go?"

Vincent ate another fork load of fish. "That's the problem. But more of a problem is the imminence and the immensity of the impending disaster. The government daren't admit that the city is improperly prepared. It daren't tell the people that millions will be killed."

"I've seen an estimate that only mentions a hundred thousand or so."

"Exactly," exclaimed Vincent, almost with triumph. "That figure is pure propaganda. Sheer nonsense. All this talk about earthquake-proof buildings is rubbish. The floating foundations of the skyscrapers and all that. It hasn't been proved that they won't crash. And they will, like a house of cards." He lifted a hand and dropped it on to the table. "And what about the people traveling squashed together in the subways? The power will fail. They'll be trapped like miners in a collapsed shaft. And who's going to dig them out? No one. There won't be anyone to rescue them. People in the streets will be killed by flying glass or falling masonry."

"But, Vincent, the quake might happen at night; then it wouldn't be so bad, would it?"

I was given another of Vincent's scowls. "It can happen at any time, in the rush hour, at midday like the Yokohama earthquake in 1923, at midnight. Whenever it happens millions will die."

"If you are so certain of such a catastrophe occurring soon, at any moment, why do you stay here? You've nearly reached retirement age. You could leave at the end of this academic year, if you wanted to. You've put in enough years to get your pension."

The waiter removed our plates. Vincent had only eaten half his dish. He lit another cigarette. I felt like mentioning the risk of lung cancer, but I didn't.

"Why do I stay?"

"Yes, why do you stay? Why does anyone stay if they don't have to?"

"Because I am like the Japanese." He paused, threw me a challenging look and declared, "I love danger."

The waiter brought the dessert menu. "Would you like apple pie à la mode? That's what I'm going to have."

"No, thanks. You know what's happened to the apple crop in the north, in the Tohoku district, don't you?"

"No. I don't. But whatever's happened to it this hotel seems to have managed to procure some apples. What about apple pie?"

"No, thanks. Just coffee."

I ordered apple pie for myself and coffee for both of us.

"What did happen to the apple crop in Tohoku?" I asked, pleased to be off the subject of earthquakes.

"Complete destruction. Absolute disaster. Caused by the unusual number of typhoons this year. Do you realize that not only the apples but most of the orchards are a complete write off?"

"I didn't know about it."

Vincent gave me one of his accusatory stares, as if I had been responsible for the calamity. "Do you realize that many of the apple growers and their wives have had to abandon their farms and go off in search of menial work in the towns?"

"No, I hadn't realized this. But you and I can do nothing about it, can we? If I knew an apple farmer in Tohoku, I could send him a letter of sympathy, but I don't. Do you have friends who are apple farmers?"

"No," Vincent admitted.

"Then why the—" I was going to say, "Why the hell do you concern yourself with the problems of the apple growers in Tohoku when there are lots of greater problems in the world?" But I didn't.

I had had enough of Vincent's forecasts and reports of doom, but I didn't want our annual lunch to end in discord.

When we had finished our coffee, we went our different ways. As I was walking towards my rented box of an apartment, I remembered that two years before when I was in Tokyo some expert had predicted that an earthquake would occur in the capital between the second and the fifth of December. I heard indirectly that Vincent had paid a visit to Kyoto over that period. I might have reminded him of this when he bragged about loving danger. Perhaps it was as well I hadn't recalled this fact. Deflating egos doesn't do much good.

 *John Haylock was born in Bournemouth, England, and educated at Aldenham School in France and at Pembroke College, Cambridge University. During most of World War II he was a liaison officer with the Greek Army. He has taught in Baghdad and Tokyo and traveled extensively. From 1965-1969 he wandered in Asia, Egypt, Morocco and Europe and came to rest in Cyprus for five years. In 1984 he retired from his university post in Japan but returns to visit in Japan each autumn. Mr. Haylock writes short stories, novels, reviews and articles. Best known in Great Britain, his writing reflects his erudition, good humor and the breadth of his travels. Over the years several of his stories have appeared in SSI.*

"Why? What had she done to them?"

Milkmoney

BY MEHRDAD NABILI

IF it were not for the fact that there had been a death in the family, one would have thought everything was as it should be in the Hamdi household. And that was the bizarre thing about it.

The memorial service was to be held that very evening and yet there was not a sound, not a movement to be discerned from the house. No chairs being carted in for the people who would be coming, no dais for the mullah to sit on and chant the Koran through the night and say a few words about Karbela and the martyrdom of Hossein once in awhile and about the calamity in the household. To a society weaned on mourning, that was inconceivable and the whole neighborhood felt cheated and went about its business pouting and in silence.

Those more in touch with the affairs of the day knew, however, that there would not be a memorial service. Not for someone placed before a firing squad by the order of the Revolutionary Court. To have as many as three relatives walk into your house under these circumstances would be open dissent, an act of rebellion against the Islamic Republic, itself punishable by death. Nothing was said about any of this, of course, in the same way that nothing was said about the execution itself. Or about the arrest before the execution or the whereabouts of the arrested person during those interminable days when your breath turned into a blind knot in the base of your throat and you wished, wished he or she had been hit by a car and was in the hospital or even dead. Anything but the dreaded and inevitable thought. And in the end all you ever received was a telephone call or a message, indirectly delivered, for you to go to Evin Prison and "take delivery of what was yours." Nothing was said even when the sack-wrapped body was handed over to you and you handed over, as if in exchange and in gratitude, a certain sum of money, specified but unspoken, to cover costs. Outside, it was known, though, that the money was the price of the bullets spent on the person you had taken delivery of and that you were expected to bury your dead in privacy and in silence.

It was under similar conditions and with similar unspoken stipulations that Judge Hamdi had been given delivery of the remains of his only daughter almost seventy hours earlier.

He had received the message on the telephone in a semi-coded fashion, but had grasped the meaning of it immediately. He had not said a word to his wife all day. It would have been folly to do so. Monireh, his wife, was no ordinary tear-bag like most Persian women, but despite her great decorum and self-control, she was not made for this kind of slapping about and would, inevitably, break down. And one thing they could not afford to do, under the circumstances, was to break down, either of them. Not that weeping and wailing and beating your chest and pulling your hair out was anything strange or uncommon to Persians generally and in these unholy times particularly; but he did not want to give those blood-thirsty bastards the pleasure of knowing how much they had hurt him.

Late in the afternoon, he had dressed himself in a three-piece suit and put on his best tie. He had done this on purpose and with a vengeance. He wanted to be quite distinguishable from the rubble who had until yesterday been more fashionably dressed than the mannequins in Paris shop windows and who now went about with pretentious stubbles, in shirts without collar turn-downs, buttoned to the top, filth rimming the cuffs, abusing the air they walked about in with the sour stench of stale sweat. This, particularly, was the time to dress up and present yourself clean-shaven and well groomed, your proud tie shouting out that you were not one of them but a true-blooded *taaghouti*, a spawn of the devil, and proud of it.

He had got into his car all by himself and driven up Pahlavi Avenue (now re-named Vali-e-Asr), turned off west into the foothills of the Alborz Mountains and arrived at Evin just as the sun was setting. There were still a good many people there, huddled around the great metal gate; but then there were always some people there day and night, waiting. Waiting to be the last at night to ask a question to which they knew they would not receive the courtesy of an answer; waiting to be the first at the break of day, hoping that somehow, through a slip somewhere, they would glean some information about someone they had somehow lost.

"Hamdi," he announced himself to the self-important urchin on the other side of the grill with an Uzi submachine gun slung under his arm. The lad could hardly have been more than twelve, but then it wasn't really he guarding the gate but the Uzi under his arm. And the shorter the fuse behind that, the better it would suit the purposes of the occasion. "Filthy bastards," he kept whispering to himself, "filthy bastards." And he waited. After a good hour and a half, the fully-bearded face of a man appeared at the grill and shouted out his name. When he presented himself at the gate the man, fire spouting out of his eyes, looked him up and down with all the hatred in the world and then the gates opened a crack to let him in.

It was so dark inside he could hardly see anything. He was led through a number of corridors and rooms, large and small, and then stopped in front of what he could barely make out to be another metal gate with another grill in it. The bearded man banged on the gate with his fist for some time and ultimately the grill opened and words were exchanged. After a few minutes the gate creaked and he was led through.

His heart had moved all the way up into his head and now filled the space between his ears, thumping away like a huge jungle drum over whose pounding he could hardly hear anything. The field of his vision had narrowed down to two mere spots, as if he had been fitted with blinkers. Numb and drained of all energy he followed the shadow in front of him, not really in touch with what was happening but trying all the while to walk with steady gait and straight back.

He almost walked into the man in front of him when they finally stopped. Through the increasing darkness and the haze which was now where his mind should have been, he got the impression that he was in an expansive hall. He could feel this more than see it. What he did see was a score or so of what looked like over-sized mail bags scattered at their feet. Other than that, nothing. There was a strange smell of rot over-ridden by carbolic acid and it was so strong it made your throat burn.

Some shuffling about on what gave the impression of being a tiled floor and some whisperings back and forth; then:

"This is your one."

He stood there, thinking for a minute that he was going to faint but pulling himself together enough to stop his knees from buckling under him. He was at a total loss as to what he should do or say.

"Do you want to identify the body?" It was the same voice, presumably of the bearded man who had brought him in.

Not being able to depend upon his own vocal chords, he threw his head up and back in a jerk, the way Persians shake their heads *No*.

"Sign this, then, and the body'll be delivered to you outside. You have means of transport, I presume?"

He took the bit of paper shoved into his left hand and signed it as best he could with the pencil stub that the man had held out to him. The man said something to whomever he had spoken to before, turned, and started ahead of him in the direction from which they had come.

Once outside, he made his way back to his car in what had once been one of the most sought-after satellite towns of Teheran, now abandoned because of its proximity to the notorious prison and turned into its parking lot. He got into the car, slung his arms over the steering wheel, leaned his head on them and only then began to shake as if he were being torn apart by a massive attack of malaria. It was late summer and in Teheran temperatures still rose above a hundred in the afternoons; yet the whole of his body shook as if his veins had been filled with liquid hydrogen.

After endless minutes, when all his insides seemed to have been shaken out, he fell back onto the back-rest, limp as a soaked rag. Finally—he had no idea after how long—he found enough energy to start the car and drive back to the prison gate. It was pitch-dark now and if the two men from the prison had not in some mysterious way identified him, he would never have seen them. They made signs to him to open up the trunk and when he did, they unceremoniously dumped into the car the sack they had brought with them.

In a haze he drove further west along the narrow road winding through the foothills until he got to Mekanir, then down south all the way to Shahyad Square (now Shohada) onto the autobahn heading west out of Teheran towards Karaj.

He had thought it all out. He was going to go to the little garden that he (like many middle class Persians) had outside the city, and bury her there. It was not legal and it was against all religious convention, but what, he had said to himself, was legal any more these days and what was there left at the hands of these sons of bitches of the religion he had believed in for a lifetime? Had they not turned every bit of this once peaceful land into a graveyard? And would they not, in a year or two, sell every graveyard to fill their own pockets? No, he would bury her outside of the law, outside of the religion so fouled by them, under the open stars that were still God's. And he would let her grow out again from the sealed soil as the flowers of her own innocence.

He was shaken out of his thoughts by the car rolling about and he realized he was doing almost a hundred and eighty kilometers. He slowed down. He was near the end of the autobahn anyway. Poor autobahn, once designed to go through the mountains all the way to the Caspian, now not only abandoned just outside Karaj, forty kilometers from Teheran, but already in rack and ruins, with potholes big enough to accommodate the whole of your car. He took the last exit out and in less than ten minutes was at the little half-acre garden tucked away in the midst of all the larger ones now taken over by the mullahs or the ragamuffins.

At the top of the treed lane he turned his lights out. He did not want to attract undue attention. Fortunately the gardens in the immediate vicinity of his little summerhouse were all so big, people would hardly bother to venture out this time of the night even to feed their ravenous curiosity. He let the car roll most of the way to his own plot, got out, quietly opened the gate and drove in.

The little two-room bungalow stood to the right of the gate as you entered so that you parked on a patch of asphalt directly in front of the door that led into it as soon as you were inside the gate. Not a very imaginative or appetizing bit of planning, but the most economical in so far as it left most of the plot for its original purpose—that of creating an orchard—and saved a good deal of paving work.

He did not go into the bungalow first. Instead he walked past it, turned right round its far corner and opened the door of the little shed built there, attached to the house, to hold tools and gardening necessities. He knew his way around the place well enough and soon found what he was after: his gardening boots and overalls, some vinyl sheeting, a pick and a short-handled shovel. He then went into the house, took off his jacket and trousers, hung them on a chair, pulled on the overalls, and changed his shoes for the gardening boots. He went out, picked up the plastic sheeting, the shovel and the pick, and walked to the far side of the little orchard.

In the late summer, the cluster of apple trees with their fruit fully ripe smelled like cider in the evening air. He made his way to the one standing in the little clearing in the midst of the trees and put down what he had brought with him. He stood there looking at the old, mother-tree, remembering how he had planted it, the first tree on the barren plot of land he had just bought, sixteen years ago on Jena's first birthday; how he had later made it stand apart from the other trees by planting around it and creating that little clearing; how he had made a point of throwing Jena's birthday parties in the garden under that tree every year. And now Jena was dead and the tree seemed old and tired.

He took up the pick and broke the little patch of earth on the far side. That would do very well. It was on the out-of-the-way side, nearer the garden wall, and yet under the spreading tree that she had loved. He put the pick down to shovel the earth out and then went back to the pick once again. The soil was well-packed and dry. There had not been any rain for months. Not that there ever was, this time of the year. And you only got your water-share once every month when the *mirab* would divert the main stream at the head of the road partly into the little hand-dug brook that ran down the side of your lane and into your garden.

By the time he had dug a hole big enough for his purpose, the sweat was boiling out of every pore in his skin and his heart was pounding. He was not young any more and he had not done this kind of thing in decades. He stood there for a minute to wipe the sweat off his brow, then started towards the car.

The boot would not open and he could not understand why until he realized he had put the wrong key into the lock. I must be nervous, he said to himself as he felt his way around the keys on the ring in the dark. Finally, he had the boot open and bent into it. He got hold of what he thought were the two ends of the sack and pulled, but the sack would not budge. It felt as if it had been filled with lead. He braced himself and slid one arm under it, wrapping the other round the top, and raised the sack using every strand of muscle in his body.

The contents of the sack had no particular form. He had expected to feel the contour of a human body inside; instead what he could make out was a knotted tree-trunk. He had never held or even touched a dead body before in his life and the realization came like a bolt of lightning to him: the bastards had not bothered to stretch the body out and rigor mortis had set in as it lay crumpled. As if in revulsion, every drop of blood in him rose to fill his head and with it he felt rising in him a mute cry of anger and anguish that came with the blood from every distant fibre of his existence and would surely tear his vocal chords out and shatter his skull. He stood there, rooted to the ground, turned into granite, for he did not know how long. Then he went limp all over and sank to the ground, the sack still in his arms. And for the first time since this horrid nightmare had begun, he let open the portals of his mind and allowed himself to face the fact that he was holding what had once been his beautiful, dark-haired little girl, white as the snow-tipped Damavand in moonlight, tender as the first apple-blossom that adorned the garden in spring. And as he clung to the shapeless form in the sack, the first sob broke in his throat and the first tear rolled down his tired face.

For what seemed an eternity he sat huddled there, holding Jena's body close to his chest and rocking it from side to side while tears washed down his face and soaked the sack-cloth. Then—he did not know after how long—he returned to himself and to the reality of the night around him.

With every care now, he carried the corpse to the shallow grave he had dug. For a minute, he stood there in two hearts.

"No. I will not," he said out loud, and his voice sounded alien to his own ears. "Whatever respect those murdering fiends may have denied her, I will not deny her mine. I will not look at her in her moment of weakness and inability."

He put the sack down, took the vinyl sheeting and covered the inside of the hole with it, leaving the corners stretched out over the ground above. Carefully, he lowered the sack into the open mouth of the grave. He took the wedding ring off his finger and placed it in a hollow in the sack. Then he folded the vinyl sheeting over the body, picked up the shovel and started piling the earth back in.

The late summer afternoon had worn itself out into a close, heat-ridden evening and Monireh had still not come down.

As he sat alone in the near-darkness of the sitting room downstairs with its curtains drawn and its light waiting to be switched on, he thought she had taken it very well. Despite the fact that she had wept herself all dry and kept herself cooped up in her room most of the time. She is an exceptional woman, he thought. Anybody else would've torn all her hair out and screamed the whole neighborhood in. Poor thing. He wished they had had Jena years earlier. Then it would not have been too late to have at least one other child who could now help her bear the pain. Perhaps, if they had had her earlier, she would have been at an age now when she would not have got herself into their clutches anyway.

He had gone straight into her room when he got back from Karaj at three in the morning, having made up his mind to tell her. He could, of course, have pretended there had been no telephone call. They had been ignorant of the girl's whereabouts for a good twenty days—formally ignorant that is—and he could have let it go on like that for a couple of weeks more. But he had made up his mind to tell her. He would have to in the end, and she would be even more hurt then for having been kept in the dark. And she knew anyway—about her being in prison, that is. He was certain she knew. The same way he did. People did not vanish without a clue in Iran the way they did in South America. Young folk did not leave home or run away as they did in Europe. And what crime there was did not all that often include disappearing acts. He knew. It was his business as a judge to know. In these troubled times, if anyone was not heard from three days running, you could be certain he or she was in Evin.

That was inevitably the place almost everyone was taken to these days, even though Evin was supposed to be the top security prison reserved for political prisoners and those tried and found guilty of serious crime. But then all crime was serious in these turbulent times and all prisoners were political, for revolutionary zeal demanded it so. And the revolutionary thirst for blood did not much care how it was quenched nor from what quarter. There was no logic to the lunacy, no method to the madness. "The Imam" was as much of an excuse, as much of a scapegoat, as the Shah had been before him. The Revolutionary Council was as ineffectual and as malleable as the Parliament had been which it had in a way replaced. And what was happening, the indiscriminate executions, the pillaging, the confiscation of private property, was neither with Khomeini's blessings nor at the Revolutionary Council's behest. The fact of the matter was that if you had somebody who did not like you—and who was there who didn't have at least one such skeleton in his cupboard?—you could be had before a "komiteh" somewhere, summarily sentenced and delivered to Evin. And the chances of anybody ever coming out of that black hole were not much better than Khomeini and the Shah kissing and making up. Blood had to be let, and any excuse would do.

"Yes, she has taken it very well. Thank God for that. Thank God for her. She is an exceptional woman."

His little girl would have made an exceptional woman too, if they had let her. But they hadn't. They had plucked her like the tender flower that she was, murdered her, wasted her. Why? What had she done to them? She was nobody's enemy. She didn't want a share of their filthy loot or their filthy power. She had even supported them at one stage, in the beginning, out of her innocence and her lack of experience with life. Then why...?

He suddenly stopped in his mind's tracks. "A fine fool you are, my friend," he said to himself, "always so wise and knowledgeable to others yet so utterly devoid of sense and reason unto yourself. Who was it a second ago giving that sermon of rational understanding about the mechanics of the revolution, calmly expounding the rationale behind what was happening in this God-forsaken hell-hole, and how and why it was happening? You fly off your rust-eaten handle every time anybody questions your brilliant analysis of things and yet it never crosses your mind to pay any heed to what you sincerely wish others had sense enough to accept. What was that brilliant expose a minute ago about there being no rhyme or reason to any of the things that were happening?"

His self-interrogation was cut short by the sound of Monireh's footsteps down the bare travertine stairs.

"Morteza?" her voice came searching down the hall. "Are you there?"

"Yes, my love, I'm here. Come on in."

"Why are you sitting in the dark? Why haven't you turned the lights on?"

"Turn them on as you come in. I was just sitting here, thinking."

She did not turn the chandelier on at the door but went round in the dark and switched on the standard lamp in the corner. Even at that, he winced as if stung and shut his eyes. He felt her sit next to him on the sofa. Poor thing, he thought. She must still be in terrible pain. She wouldn't have come and sat next to him if she weren't. It wasn't done. His heart went out to her and he wanted to take her in his arms and hold her but he stopped himself. That wasn't done either. Not in traditional Persian families. No, that's not true, he thought. From all accounts Persians did that very openly before Islam. Damn Islam, he thought.

Morteza Hamdi, retired Judge of the Court of Appeal, had always considered himself a good Moslem, as had everybody else who knew him. Up until the advent of Ayatollah Khomeini, that is, and the barbarity he and his followers had brought with them. Then, like many thousands of other people, he had been shaken awake to the reality of what Islam, at least Khomeini's version of it, meant. He had until then found strength in his belief. He was certain he could not have done half the things he had, as a judge, if he had not had that belief. And that is why he had asked to be retired after the first year of the revolution. What he had seen done during that year by the mobs, by the so-called "komitehs" or people's courts, even by the Islamic judges—especially by the Islamic judges—had shattered his confidence in what he had so boldly done all through his years on the bench. How could he have been right leaning on his belief if this was what his belief meant? He had never been a religious fanatic, but he had believed strongly enough to feel sure-footed in what he did, in the judgments he passed. Now, the whole of that certitude was gone and he could no longer sit in judgment of anything or anyone without going through the pains of purgatory. He had to give up.

He felt her move and, as if in denunciation of all tradition, willfully put his hand out and got hold of hers. She leaned sideways without moving and placed her head on his shoulder. She was utterly still, completely limp, and he remembered the young girl, brimful of life and bursting with energy, who had come into his life those many years ago as his bride. He put his arm round her shoulder and felt her quietly sobbing.

"Don't," he said, tears rolling down his own face. "We mustn't. For her sake. She was very young but she knew what she was doing and she'd not want us to degrade what she gave her life for out of our selfishness."

"What did she give her life for?" he then asked himself, silently. He remembered the first time she got into an argument with him over Khomeini. That was during the strikes when everybody was out there in the streets watching the banks burn and people happily queued outside the little oil depot for hours, waiting to see if they could get a gallon of kerosene to keep themselves warm on. And this in the country which was the third biggest producer of oil in the world.

"What's happened to this race of people?" he asked, addressing nobody in particular, over the top of his afternoon newspaper.

"I don't know, I'm sure," said his wife, sitting with her legs pulled up under her on an armchair across the room from him.

Jena was reading some book or other in the far corner. These days there were no lessons or homework to do. The schools were all closed, the universities were all closed, everything was closed. The only racket still in full swing was politics, and to politics everyone had turned.

"Maybe this race of people has finally had enough and wants out."

He had seldom felt such sharpness in her voice and he said, smiling:

"Ho, ho, ho! So we too are growing political hair, are we? Tell me, Mrs. Gandhi, and how is burning down banks and standing in queues going to get us out of whatever it is we want to get out of?"

Monireh looked up at him with a shade of reproach in her eyes, as if to say leave the child alone. He winked at her to say he was only pulling her leg.

"What are ordinary people in the street to do against an ogre like the Shah, then? Anyway, it's not them starting the fires, it's Khomeini's followers. And they have to stand in queues because the workers in the oil industry have gone on strike on Ayatollah Khomeini's orders. All the people are doing is to make it all look more serious, to give it more publicity."

He was surprised to see how seriously she took it all. He was also surprised at how much she knew about what was happening; and she was only fifteen. He felt sad. Why was it that every Persian child became so conscious of and so involved in politics? European children didn't; American children didn't. Was it something in third-world upbringing? He had never been involved in politics and he thought he had brought her up in a household free of the curse. Or of any kind of proclivity, for that matter. Did the world outside have so much influence on a child?

"And what are the people, whoever they are, going to do when and if they succeed in getting their 'out' as you call it? When they have got rid of the ogre? Do they think things are going to be any better or any different?"

"They think things are going to be a lot better when Ayatollah Khomeini comes."

He looked her in the eye for the first time and said, seriously:

"It is the Shah that is the only problem in this country then, is it? And everything will be sorted out once he's gone?"

"Given a decent ruler, yes."

"So you've joined the hordes of ignoramuses who think it's the ship that controls the sea it floats on, have you?" he said rather sadly.

She seemed to sense the disappointment in his voice and when she spoke, her own was warm and full of love.

"I haven't joined anything, Daddy. I am just repeating what they say in school and in the street. I'm sorry."

"Don't be sorry, my pet, just careful. The problems the world has are not as simple as people want to believe. Or as easy to correct as intellectuals want us to think so they can have a cause to fight for and a campaign to start."

"But don't you think things would be different if the Shah left and somebody else took charge?" she asked, not in argument but genuinely wanting to see what he thought.

"Somebody else meaning Khomeini, whoever he is?"

"No. He doesn't want to be involved with politics; he doesn't want to rule. He is a man of God. He wants nothing to do with the/world and its affairs. He has said so himself many times."

"Do you really believe that? Do you honestly think the man's sitting there outside Paris, getting his cronies to set fire to the financial institutions of this country, to destroy things and kill people, without wanting anything out of it? He must be raving mad if he is. And anyway, even if he is the holy spirit you and your friends think he is, do you think your fellow countrymen are going to let him remain that? Do you for one minute think that this race of idol-makers is going to go to all the trouble of risking its neck to get rid of the Shah and bring this Khomeini person in and then let him go to Qum and sit in the madrasah there and have nothing to do with anything? You have a great, great deal to learn about your fellow countrymen, my love, if that's the way you see things."

She remained silent and he felt he had been talking down to her. So he said:

"Anyhow, that's as it may be. What I'm more interested in is to know how you feel about the whole thing."

She thought a minute and then replied:

"Well, to be quite honest, I don't feel anything. Not for myself; not really. I know how my friends feel about it all and I empathize with them; but I don't have any particular feelings of my own. I think there are a lot of things wrong with this country. I think there are a lot of things wrong with the Shah and with the government. But I tend to agree with what you have often said: that you can't set things right simply by replacing them with other things and hoping for the best."

Was that what she had given her life for? Something she had no definite feeling about? Out of empathy for others? No, of course not. Things hadn't stayed like that, as he remembered.

Monireh moved slightly, and brought him back to the present.

"Shall I go and get the coffee started?" he offered. "Mojtaba and Mehri should be here soon."

Mojtaba and Mehri were her brother and his sister, the only two people whom they had told and who were coming over for a memorial service of sorts on the third day of Jena's death. Nobody else. Not even Monireh's mother. They couldn't take the risk. They both knew she would go into such hysterics she would wake the dead. Generations of tradition had instilled in her as in most other Persians that it was the epitome of disrespect towards the dead if you did not, and unkindness and animosity towards those left behind. So many generations that by now it had become second nature. They could not afford to have any of that. In fact, they had laid down the condition that silence and decorum would be observed before they had agreed for Mojtaba and Mehri to come over.

"No," she replied. "I'll get up and see to it in a minute. Do you want to fetch the Koran?"

He thought for a minute.

"No. Not the way I had to bury her. And anyway, it'll take me a bit of time to get over all this and come to terms with the Koran again. It'll take this country quite a bit of time to do that too. At the moment, I don't want any of it."

She did not say anything. In a moment she got up and headed for the kitchen to prepare the coffee. She forgave him for his irreverence and could not help but smile inwardly at his mistake about the coffee. How was he to know? After all, he was only a man. A good man and a gentle one. A great deal better than most Persian husbands in so far as he did not look at it as his God-given right to sit down and expect to be spoon-fed. But a man all the same. To him, coffee was when you switched the kettle on and poured the water, once it was boiling, on the coffee in your cup. Rather like tea. How was he to know that the coffee you served when someone was dead was a different kind of coffee?

She took down the little tinned copper mug with the long handle in which you threw together the extra-fine, dark coffee, the cold water and the sugar and brought the whole thing slowly to the boil to make Turkish coffee.

She thought of her little girl and a pang shot through her. She could still not really believe she was dead. She just could not understand what was happening. The only thing that told her all was not as it should be was the pain she felt every time she thought of the girl. How could she be dead? Why should she be dead? Her husband had not told her much except that he had taken delivery of a corpse from somebody and had buried it somewhere. As far as she was concerned it could have been anybody's corpse. He hadn't checked, had he?

"I'm not actually going to do the coffee," she raised her voice, "just get everything in order."

"As you think."

She took her time and he sat there thinking what he was going to say to his sister and Mojtaba. What was there to say? They had arrested her, supposedly tried her as they did hundreds of others a day, and shot her. That he had already told them over the 'phone. And that was more than he himself knew. All he really knew was that somebody had called him and told him to go to Evin and take delivery of a corpse, and he had. Nobody had explained anything and he had not asked for any explanation. It would have been futile to. Others had tried. Individuals and individual rights had never meant anything in Iran and they meant even less now. He wondered whether they really meant any more even in the so-called Western democracies.

The front gate bell rang and, getting up, he shouted, "I'll get it."

The little coffee cups lay abandoned and mourning on the low table, the corners of their mouths stained with the black tears of their contents. The little rose patterns down the handles and round the rims of the little saucers, instead of lending a note of optimism, brought more solemnity to the occasion.

They had been sitting there, facing one another in complete silence, for the last twenty minutes. Judge Hamdi was not an easy person to talk to at the best of times, not only because he was the senior member of the family but also because he was a tranquil and measured man in front of whom you did not want to make a fool of yourself by opening your mouth too often. Not that he would be unkind or say anything disparaging if you did. In fact, he would invariably turn your words into something meaningful which would make you sound quite important. But whereas others would look at you with admiration for the clever point you had made, you yourself, unless you were an utter fool, would realize all the more the stupidity of your own original remark.

When they had first walked in at the gate, Mehri and Mojtaba had just embraced him and not said a word. Morteza Hamdi had a way of communicating with people without having to say much and those who had spent any time with or around him very soon learned to do the same. Inside the house, when they had come face to face with Monireh, they had merely uttered a few words in simple condolence and then checked themselves, not wanting to go too far. Over the thimble-sized cups of thick, scalding and syrup-sweet black coffee that Monireh brought in after preliminary Persian niceties had been bandied about for the polite and appropriate length of time, Mehri had made bold enough to break the ice.

"Agha-dadash, why?" she had asked, desperately trying to stop the tears she felt were welling up in her eyes. She always addressed him as agha-dadash, for he was her eldest brother.

He looked at her, his normally calm, doleful eyes now deep pools of liquid pain.

"I wish I knew. Is there any why or wherefore to any of the savagery these people have been wreaking on each other and us? She hasn't been the only one. They're killing people off by the hundreds every day. Does there have to be a reason? Any reason besides the fact that man is the most blood-thirsty animal in this jungle?"

His voice was as calm and as mellow as the close, balmy late-summer air. He might have been talking to a friend about the weather.

"What had they arrested her for?" asked Mojtaba, drawing upon all his courage.

"I don't know. It's not as if people are arrested, you know. An arrest is an act of law which can be carried out by only those authorized by law to carry it out. What is happening here today is more like abduction. You could arrest anyone you wanted. All it takes is for you to be in sham fatigues and behind a filthy beard. A gun over your shoulder would help but isn't essential. You can arrest anyone and take them to any of the prisons or *komitehs* and they'd do the rest."

"But they have to have some sort of excuse, don't they?"

"Oh, there's no shortage of excuses. Anybody who ever knew you in your life could have an excuse to hand you in or turn informer, even your own children. For has the Imam not proclaimed it a religious duty for all and sundry to inform against those doing or even uttering anything against the Islamic Republic?"

"Could it have been one of her Mujahedin friends?" asked his wife, more to draw him out than to suggest anything.

"Could have been, but I don't think it was. Raw and ill-informed they may be, but traitors to their friends and their cause they are not. I just don't know. All I know is that like all children her age she was full of sweet dreams about life and the world. She believed, as they all do, in original good instead of the original sin religion teaches. She believed there is sanity and order in nature if it is left to its own devices and that man is fundamentally good. She held that it is only because of the way we, the older generation, run things that the world is the horrid place it is, that there does not have to be pain and inequality. She believed that nature is fair and kind and gives everybody an equal chance. There is no way you can make a child of that age see otherwise, accept that nature is not fair, that it does not give everybody an equal chance, that if there is no original sin, there is no original benevolence either. They have not lived long enough or experienced the world enough to know that one thing is the inevitable outcome of another, that you cannot stop anything in mid-flight to turn it into something else. And who would want to do that anyway? Who could be short-sighted enough to want to deny the world the fresh breath of youth with its idealism? It is a boring enough world even with them in it. We've seen to that."

He had not changed his tone or pitch during all that, just his pace. And now he stopped and turned round to his wife.

"Are you going to give us another cup of that coffee, khanom?"

While she was gone they all sat in silence and Mehri lit a cigarette. He and his wife did not smoke, but they did not mind others doing so in their house. She, Jena, had once asked them if they would mind if she took up smoking and he had answered no, why should they? And she had never taken to it.

With fresh little cups of coffee in their hands, Mehri said:

"But she was never one of them, was she? I mean one of the Mujahedin?"

"No. She dreamed their dreams but did not share their dogma. And anyway, she was not a one to join campaigns and movements. She wanted things to get better and, like them, made the mistake of thinking that Khomeini and his lot wanted the same thing too. Then, when they saw the reality of the Islamic Republic and discovered how they had been duped, they all turned away, and that was when they started being arrested and tortured, then killed. No, she wasn't one of them but she wanted what she innocently thought they wanted, and she was willing to stand up and have her say."

"You mean to say they killed her because of what she said?" It was Mojtaba speaking this time, astonishment washing over his face like a wave.

"I don't know. I'm only conjecturing. No, not so much because of what she said as because of the way she said it, I suppose. If you have an obsessive conviction you can't stand conviction in someone else. If you have a dream of your own you hate dreamers of other dreams. Khomeini's followers think they've stood up against the Shah and drowned him in their own blood to create the Utopia they call the Islamic Republic. How can they stand the treachery, the affront, of anyone negating what they've done by asking for another Utopia?"

"You mean to say she was a political activist and was campaigning against them?"

"No. No she wasn't even interested in politics."

"What then? What would they want with her then? Why would they want to kill her?"

"Because she had a mind. If there's one thing dogma can't stand it's a mind. Because mind is logic and logic is the strongest antidote against dogma. And she had an even worse blight: she spoke what was on her mind, no matter what."

He could see they had not really understood him. How could they? How could a race that never ever said what it thought understand the phenomenon of someone who did? How could one who mistook what he said for what he thought conceive of a mind within its own right?

The front gate bell rang just as Mehri was opening her mouth to say something.

"I'll see who it is," said Mojtaba, jumping to his feet.

He was back after what seemed like a long stretch of

conversation, his usual forlorn look on his face.
"It's one of these characters. He wants a word with you, Agha Morteza."
"One of which characters? And what does he want to have a word with me about?"
"One of these bearded, rifled characters. Probably a Pasdar. And he won't say what he wants to talk about."
Judge Hamdi looked at his wife as if to see if he could find a clue on her face.
"What would a Revolutionary Guard want with me at this time of night, I wonder?"
"Shall I tell him to come in the morning?"
"No, ask him to come in. Might as well get it over with right now. Khanom, will you and Mehri go upstairs while I see this person?"
He was not worried, just puzzled. These bearded, gun-toting people in fatigues came in a number of groups, each with its own designation, all self-created and self-appointed. They all claimed to be there to look after the interests of the Islamic Republic and to keep the peace. In effect what they did was to interfere in everything and try to hack a livelihood out for themselves. Normally they did not come knocking politely at your door, asking to have a word with you: they assailed your house in groups without warning, broke down your door if you lived in a flat or climbed over your wall if you had a house; came in, introduced themselves with the butts of their guns, foul mouthed and intimidated you, knocked your furniture about, broke what they could, took what they wanted and left the questioning to their colleagues in the *komitehs* to which they dragged you. He knew all that, but he was not the kind of man to worry about this sort of thing. He was just puzzled.
The man who stood at the door to the living room, cleaning his boots on an imaginary door mat, his head down, his G3 hanging from his shoulder, was no better or worse than any of his kind. Without his jet-black, full beard he could even be said to be handsome in a Persian sort of way. He tried to look deadly serious and tough, and only managed to appear constipated and ill-tempered

like all the rest of them.

"Are you Judge Hamdi?" he asked, trying hard not to let any politeness or concern show in his voice.

"Yes."

"Are you Jena Hamdi's father?"

The judge looked at him with renewed interest and compounded perplexity. Who was this unkempt, ill groomed lad with a typical south-Tehran accent and how did he know his daughter? As if he had read the question on his face, the man said:

"I am one of the Pasdars at Evin prison."

He came forward with a half crumpled, dirt-gray envelope held in front of him in his right hand. He bent low and placed the envelope on the side table near him, then backed all the way to the door.

"I come from a decent Moslem family. It is custom among us to pay a token sum of money to the mother of a virgin bride. This is not much but it is all I have and I should like Jena's mother to have it. I took the girl in temporary marriage on her last night and I don't want to be answerable to God on the day of judgment for not having paid the *milkmoney* due her mother."

He turned round and, before Morteza Hamdi's fog-ridden mind had had time enough to register the significance of what he had said, he was gone.

Born in Tehran, in 1933, Mehrdad Nabili spent his childhood in Afghanistan and India, went to an English school and then to London University. He has a B.A. in literature, a B.S. in economics, an M.Ed. in education and a Ph.D. in psychology. He has been a banker, teacher, university professor and radio broadcaster. He writes, "Over and above everything I have been a writer, translator and journalist." He is a well-known writer in Iran. This is his first published story in the USA. Presently, he is working in England as a writer/producer/broadcaster.

"But it was different today. Something had gone wrong."

Encounter

BY SHAMMAI GOLAN

ROSENBERG could tell what time it was by the patch of sun on his morning paper. The yellow light had reached the Letters to the Editor. Advice. Complaints. Appeals. He had read them all, as he did every day. Perhaps because Nimrod's letters were so few and far between. And now, it was time. He had been here on the bench since ten o'clock. The same as always. Sitting down with the same sigh of relief. The years of work at the factory. The constant ache in his back. The joints of his hands. His feet. They said the Jerusalem climate had an effect. The bench dug its screws into him. The morning news did nothing to alleviate his pain. He knew it almost by heart. The editorial. The News in Brief columm The Quotation for the Day. By the time he came to the readers' letters, his body was tense with anticipation of the boys' arrival.

He glanced at his watch. Just to be sure. The sun always made that yellow patch at this time of day. Still, one should check. Rectangular watch. Five years on his wrist without stopping even for a moment. Heavy and stable. Stainless steel strap. Always showing the correct time, the day of the week, the date. Every day. Tirelessly. It also illuminated the night with its glowing hands. A gift from the management on his retirement. They had assured him that a man who knew the exact time and date would never experience loneliness.

But the hands moved with maddening slowness. The patch of sun was still on the readers' letters. The boys never came early. Their school principal was probably strict. Probably made them work at their lessons even if one of their teachers was absent. Youngsters had to get used to thinking for themselves. Studying in depth. Reaching conclusions. That was the only way a person could really achieve his independence. His Nimrod used to recite the principal's words from memory. He was independent from a very early age. He used to come home late. Today, too, the boys would not turn up before he had finished reading the News in Brief. And the classified ads. But he had been cutting down on his reading over the last few days. His eyes were starting to betray him. Headaches. The heart suddenly raced. The boys never came early.

But they came at the regular time. First of all the voices, from above. From the park gate opposite their school. High tones blending with deeper ones. Boys whose voices were still breaking. There was nothing regular about them, other than the time of their arrival. And here they were, following their voices. Large limbs. Wild hair. Blue shirts. Jeans. Tumultuously taking possession of the park. Making themselves at home. Shoving and being shoved. Rolling their schoolbags. The sound of yowling cats. Screeching girls. Barking dogs. Pogrom.

Rosenberg keeps track of them over the edge of his newspaper. Over the top of his glasses. He is quite concealed in the shade of the tall pine. Receiving the softly falling pine needles on his bald head, his shoulders. The hard seat of the bench pushes up against him. He does not move. The nail-heads. The bougainvillaea at his back. Flower thorns.

The boys are coming from above. Down the wide stone steps.

Must not miss their arrival. Must not waste the moments of their coming. They have to notice him. Stop by him. Say, "Hey old man!" Then disperse. Leap boldly over the bushes. Over the rosebeds.

But no. They were eyeing him. Surrounding him. Their leader was sitting at the end of the bench. Casually. Putting down his schoolbag. Between himself and Rosenberg. Bare arm. Downy golden hairs. Long, tanned fingers. Feet curling over the soles of his sandals. His friends stand off a little. Bunched together. Like mountains enclosing Rosenberg. Rocks on all the paths. He is on his own. Furtively observing their movements. Knowing the position of each one. The threatening murmur intensifies. He merely smiles to himself. For he knows that one of them, maybe the leader sitting so close, will call out, "OK, you guys, that's enough, leave the old man alone." And they would all leave. And Rosenberg would know that he had been one of them.

But it was different today. Something had gone wrong. The leader pulled a long brown cigarette from the pocket of his jeans jacket. Thin as a nail. Someone gave him a light. A smell of incense rose on the air. Rosenberg could sense his quickening heartbeat. Here it came. The fragrant smoke encompassing him. Penetrating his nostrils. His mouth. Entering his lungs. Another boy approaches. Pushes the leader, shoves his schoolbag. "Move over!" As if chasing the leader from the bench. But Rosenberg knows it is directed at him. "The bench is for everyone!" shouts the boy, winking. His eyes are black. Shooting sparks of merriment. "Your schoolbag's in our way!" Puts out a hand, as if to move the bag. Instead, he knocks the newspaper out of Rosenberg's hands. It's hard for the old man to bend. His back. Hunching over the iron machines in the factory for thirty years. Bending twenty- and forty-millimeter iron bars, turning them on the lathe.

Nevertheless, he bent and picked up the newspaper. Again it was snatched out of his hands. Flung to the ground. Rosenberg raised his eyes. The boy was standing in front of him. One foot flicked out, close to Rosenberg's knees. Springy, balanced stance.

The boy's eyes dared him. Someone in trainers came and stepped on the newspaper. Quietly. Deliberately. Without apparent anger. Rosenberg knew that silence. Was prepared for verbal abuse. A shouted insult. He had been expecting this moment all morning. Should he get away now? The newspaper was a dead loss, anyhow. They would give him another one at the grocer's. They would wrap his two rolls, his fifty grams of hard cheese and the plastic carton of yoghurt in it. He did not do any cooking since his wife Leah died. Only tea, or coffee. He sometimes found two or three poems on the wrapping paper. Short lines. Incomprehensible. A new world. Even in poems.

The boys were becoming agitated. He could sense the agitation in their muttering. They were losing patience. One of them suggested that they should move on. Trace of alarm in his voice. Afraid of what might happen. A girl's voice adds, "Not worth it. Just an old guy having a rest." Nice girl. Jeans skirt. Hair tumbling around her cheeks. Nightingale voice.

Rosenberg roared. "Quiet, hoodlums! Just shut up!" Deep down, he hoped to stop them from going. To give them an excuse to stay. He bent to pick up the newspaper. The shreds of complaints being trampled under a shoe. Blue and white. The laces yellow. Woolen socks, too. In the middle of the heat wave, woolen socks. He almost burst out laughing. But the trainers were ominous. They stood wide, long. Size forty-four. Maybe even forty-five. Same as Nimrod. Funny boys. So young and their shoes already so big. The faintly dusty, sweaty smell. He kept his son's shoes to this very day. Mudstains on the soles. Nimrod had gone overseas to study medicine and had not come back for his shoes.

Rosenberg gave the foot a gentle nudge. As he had nudged the horse's foot in his youth. Somewhere. In the distant homeland of Mother and Father and *goyim* who spoke Polish. He whispered in Polish, "*Noga.*" Which means foot. The shoe lifted. The edge of it knocked his hand. Flexing his stricken hand, he gripped the ankle and pulled the pages from under the foot. He looked up, trying to encounter the boy's eyes. He smiled. But the boy winked at his friends and hopped on to the paper with his other foot.

Again Rosenberg bent down and grasped the foot. He could feel the vein beating in the ankle, under the sock. In the evenings, he used to kiss the tiny soles of Nimrod's feet. He would remove the little light-soled trainers, put on his floral pajamas. Nimrod would laugh, kicking his little feet and shouting, "Wanna sleep in them!" and the whole room laughed with him. The window panes, the curtains, the carpet, the lampshade. Rosenberg would cover his son's body with kisses. Now Nimrod was a well-known doctor. In the country over the sea. Sometimes, on the rare occasions when he wrote, he would include a casual photograph of his son. "Your grandson," he would write. Indeed, he resembled Nimrod. The fair shock of hair, the freckled, upturned nose.

The boy flicked his shoe again, hitting Rosenberg on the thigh, near the groin. Rosenberg, mechanically, punched the boy in the stomach.

"Zap, old man!" came the taunting cry. The boy's eyes darted around, seeking witnesses to his insult, the revenge he was about to take.

"Leave the old man alone!" called the nightingale's voice. But the others crowded closer, jostling each other. Like a train jolting its carriages in a sudden halt. The boy was standing in front of him, his hands close to the old man's chest, at throat level. Warm hands, half-hesitant, half-threatening. Rosenberg began imperceptibly to slide along the bench. The nail-heads hurt him as he slowly pushed himself backwards against the wood. The yellow paint flaked on to the seat of his pants. Making a big yellow patch. The insult surged in his heart, rose in a ball of fury to his throat. He stood up, grabbing the lapels of the boy's jacket in both hands. Good cloth. It held. He took pleasure in tensing his muscles. He still had power in his hands. Now he would show them who Old Rosenberg was. It seemed as if his whole life force was concentrated in his hands. All at once he lifted the boy off the ground. Saw with amazement the big helpless feet. The huge trainers dangled in the air. The impudent look in the boy's eyes gave way to fear. Rosenberg took a deep breath. He raised his eyes to heaven for a moment. Thankful for his great victory. Then he carefully lowered the boy.

"So you're going to be a doctor, eh?" he grinned into the boy's face. A big-time doctor!"

The prominent Israeli writer Shammai Golan was born in Poland in 1933. He experienced Nazi occupation and exile in Cyprus before entering Israel in 1947. He was educated in a kibbutz and at Hebrew University. Mr. Golan served as Israel's Cultural Attaché in Mexico (1984-1987), Chairman of the Hebrew Writers' Association (1981-1984, 1988-1991) and Chairman of the PEN World-Wide Conference held in Jerusalem in 1974. His awards include the Prime Minister's Literary Award 1991, the coveted Agnon Prize for Literature, Asher Barash Prize, ACUM Prize, Ramat-Gan Prize and the Walenrod Award of the Hebrew Writers' Association. The poet Riva Rubin, Chairwoman of the Israeli Writers in the English Language, translated the story. Mr. Golan's story "The Return" appeared in SSI No. 25.

"You realize both with pride and a sense of loss that he's now his own man."

Your Son and Ideals

BY GOH SIN TUB

WELCOME! Step right in. Into this story as it takes place.

Imagine, if you will, that this is happening to you right now. Your son is leaving you. He is going to the UK for further studies. You are driving him to Changi Airport.

You and your wife have been overwhelming him with all the dos and don'ts you can think of during the last few weeks and especially the last few days. Yet you now still rack your brains for any important advice you may have forgotten.

Suddenly for no reason you think of a line from Shakespeare and you blurt it out.

"This above all—to thine own self be true."

The silence before and after your statement gives it an unexpected emphasis which surprises you.

"Yes, Dad," he ponders and replies dutifully.

Your wife can also be seen searching her mind for any forgotten instructions of her own. She ends up repeating:

"Don't forget to ring us when you get to the hostel."

As though he would. After so many reminders it must be engraved in stone in his mind.

You go through that familiar airport farewell drill. You have done this before. With your other children who also departed overseas. Each time you go through that surge of sorrow of separation. How will he manage, studying and looking after himself as well?

You miss him already before he goes. You know you and your wife will feel the emptiness and the sudden quietness of your home for some days to come.

Nevertheless you postpone your sadness. You manage to hold back the loneliness already with you. Until he is about to check into Departure. Then, in that farewell hug, your eyes well up. He does not see it. Until he embraces his openly weeping Mum and he looks over her shoulder at you. His eyes turn red too. He is your youngest. He has been closest to you. He has never been away for long.

"Look after yourself, Jack," you say, touching his dear mop of hair with your tender hand. He's your very dearest. He may not listen to you at times but deep down you can count on his love and he always ponders on what you say and obeys you.

On the way back home you hold your wife's hand and you say to reassure her and yourself:

"Don't worry! Jack knows how to take care of himself. His NS years in the Army have made him a man."

"He's not as practical as Arthur or Bertie," replies Grace, comparing him with his much older brothers now married and settled down in the States.

You nod. Arthur and Bertie are different. They have been extroverts from childhood. As kids they were quite a handful. Boisterous. Made a lot of noise. Always running around, hyperactive, curious, involving themselves in everything within reach.

Jack has always been the opposite. Quiet, studious, serious, prefering the inner world of books and music and model airplanes. He was a bit soft. Not outgoing enough. A little too dependent.

But the Army did him good. It helped to roughen and toughen him a bit.

Nevertheless he is your youngest, your baby of the family and you still worry about him. And you feel for your wife, knowing the black abyss of her empty nest now that her last fledging has flown. Once again it comes on you, that remorse that neither you nor your wife can accompany him on this trip. Your restaurant business is really too demanding. Yes, it is such a busy time right now for the two of you. Later on, at least Grace can get away. You can manage alone. She will go to see him.

You are glad Jack has been accepted for that university course in Business Administration. It's a good and useful course. He will do well. Then he will come home and run the family business with you and your wife. His brothers are not interested. He's the one. He will take over from you.

Dear God, look after him, guide him, protect him, you pray.

The phone rings at 7 pm, Singapore time. On the dot as pre-arranged. Grace gets to it first. You listen on the extension.

He has arrived safe and sound, but he's sure sleepy, man. He has checked into his hostel. He's worried about a hitch. There are some papers he needs for university registration. He thinks he has to get them fast. He wonders if he will be allowed to start classes.

You pause. Your first thought is to fly over at once with them and help him get over the problem. But you realize quickly you only need to send the papers over.

After a few days his first letter arrives. It is very reassuring. His registration was no problem after all. He has made friends and settled down. He says he may not be able to write frequently. He has a tight schedule and has to rush around a lot. The study program is very wide.

You are anxious about his workload. But, on the other hand, you are happy he is kept busy. He will not have leisure to be lonely.

Very soon you and your wife have to bury yourselves in your work. The restaurant business is indeed a hard taskmaster. The business planning and the operational accounts take a lot of your after-work hours.

Before you know it a year has gone by. Jack seems OK, even from his meager correspondence. He says less and less, scratching out only a few hurried lines in each of his rare letters.

He's too busy, you and your wife excuse him. He has to spend time on his studies.

There are of course the occasional trunk calls. To wish you or your wife happy birthday. Occasionally it is for something special, such as someone coming over on holiday from the UK who has kindly agreed to collect from you some of his old books for him.

You and your wife also try to ring him up. But it's almost impossible to reach him in the hostel. It's hard to get through to that busy phone. When you do finally get through, the person at the other end can't be bothered to go and call Jack.

And so gradually the communication thins out between you and your son. Your wife writes him long letters in small print. You join in with your equally small print.

You talk about almost anything—family news, gossip, politics, religion, your business aspirations and so on.

From him, long episodes of silence broken by brief notes and equally brief phone calls.

He is busy in the first year so he does not come home. Your wife goes over and finds he is up to his neck in study assignments and postings for work experience.

"He's OK," she reports over the phone. "He's more pale. And thinner." Actually you find it difficult to tell any such deterioration from his photos, but a mother's sharp eyes can always see more than others and spot the slightest change in a son's well-being.

She therefore feeds him and teaches him some simple nutritious cooking while she's there. And when she gets back she begins to send him lots of food parcels, including ginseng and other good stuff.

After his second year he is scheduled to come home for his vacation but he decides to tour Europe with his friends instead. So you have not seen your son for two years now.

Mercifully time flies by fast, especially when you have two busy restaurants to run and good business keeps you both occupied. You find less time to write and even your wife has to curtail her letters. She too gets more tied up in your family business since it is booming and makes its relentless demands.

When you write, you are preoccupied with business matters and they overflow into your letters. You mention your worries whether your profits will be sustained, whether this new place just opened will take away your customers, whether your overhead will continue to leap up.

Despite all this there is mostly silence from the other end.

Sometimes you wonder what his reactions are to your letters. Does he find these items of practical business concerns interesting? No doubt. After all, he is doing Business Administration.

Another year zooms by real fast. Jack is now studying for his final examinations. He does not write at all. He has not done so for three whole months. In fleeting moments, you and your wife worry about this. You write to him to ring up. He does not.

So you write a stern letter saying he must ring up as both of you are worried sick about him, especially how he is doing in his preparations for his crucial examinations. You are now looking forward to his return home upon completion of his course so that he can enter your family business. He will be making good solid money with you.

He rings up at last. He is very sorry. He is caught up in his studies and student activities. He is studying hard but he is also involved in some important social work through the students' Community Services Society.

He's sure he's OK with his studies. Should be able to pass. No sweat. And he goes on to talk more about the social work he is doing for the handicapped.

After he rings off you begin to worry whether he is not spending too much time on such extra-curricular activities. Grace agrees with you—you should write to him about it.

You do. In your next letter you point out that the exams are more crucial to him. The sooner he passes the sooner he comes home, and the earlier he can get down to work in the family business and help you to earn even more attractive profits in your family line. There's plenty of time for social work later if one really wants to go into it.

There's a lot of money to be made here. Just waiting for him to come home. You end your letter with this strong motivational line. What more can a father say?

You do not know what impact your words have made. Because all you get is silence.

Anyway, he passes his exams. No honors. Just a pass. But that's OK. After all, he's coming home now to his own family's business.

He does not come home at once. He stays behind "to tidy up a few loose ends." A few loose ends? For one whole month?

Then one day out of the blue he pops up. He's back home in a taxi without even ringing to tell you first.

You and your wife are overjoyed to see him. He looks the same and yet somehow different. Fairer. Yes, also a bit thinner. His dear mop of hair has thinned down. He's more serious-looking than before. And definitely more independent. You realize both with pride and a sense of loss that he's now his own man. Not your boy any more.

The next evening over dinner you raise the happy prospect of his coming into your business.

"When do you want to start?"

He does not answer at once. His eyes look away. You get an ominous feeling in the stomach. Your wife's eyes tell you she's getting that sinking feeling too.

"Dad." He looks at you now straight in the eye and says: "I don't want to go into your business. Or any business."

"But, but..." you splutter, unable to find words.

"I'm really sorry, Dad and Mum. I just can't do it. My heart's not in it. I have to do my own thing...Don't you remember what you said to me as I left Singapore? Your important last words?"

You don't. Honestly, you don't.

"What you said then has remained in my head all these years. You said, 'Above all, to yourself be true.' Well, I am now being true to myself. I'll be a hypocrite if I go into business. I've changed. I'm not interested in money now. Why does it have to be money, money, all the time! There are other things more important in life. I want to reach out and help the handicapped. For me this is more meaningful than just making money!"

You are confused and stunned. Then you are angry. What stupidity is this? How can a son of yours become like this? Especially after getting a degree in Business Administration.

You lash out with your heart and your tongue. He remains unmoved. He is no longer your obedient boy. He is a stranger with his own alien stand. And he stands stubborn.

"Jack, Jack, what is all this nonsense? Think it over," you say. "Don't waste your life. You have to do something which will get you a good income. Something to give you and your future family a decent life."

"I have thought it over," he announces. "I want to return to London. I've a job offer in the St. George's School for the Deaf. I'll be a trainee teacher. I'll be working and studying at the same time. I'm taking my Diploma in Education for the Handicapped in one year. Then I'll return home and work here."

"Jack, Jack." You shake your head. "What kind of career is that? How much can you get?"

"Dad, you don't seem to understand at all. It's not the money I want. I must do what is meaningful to me. The world is too full of shallow money-minded people. Who's going to help our brothers in need? Who's going to accept the task of helping the handicapped get their chance for a life of some meaning. Someone has to do that. Someone has to make the sacrifice. To forget about money-making, about a career—and just reach out and help our fellow-men in need."

"Why the deaf, Jack?" interposes Grace, somewhat irrelevantly to the main issue.

"Mum, the deaf are the most neglected. Everyone automatically sees and feels pity for the blind. You can see that they *can't* see. So your heart goes out to them. And your money too. But the deaf seem perfectly normal. Although they are totally shut out from our world in which sound is so important. Nobody notices the deaf. In fact, people get annoyed with them because they seem stupid when they don't respond."

"Yes, that's true," Grace agrees, to your annoyance.

Jack begins to wax eloquent. "I want to help to break their sound barrier, to bring language and meaning into their world of silence."

"Yes, yes," you interrupt testily. "Quite a speech, Jack. But why you? Many people want to help the handicapped. But we can do both—pursue our business and help them as well. We can work hard, make money and then donate to the societies for the handicapped and help them that way."

"Yes, Dad, but..."

"But what?"

"That's your way. That's not my way."

You are completely flabbergasted.

Your way? His way? When did your two ways separate? Of course—in those three years in your two different worlds.

"You're too idealistic! You must come down to earth now, Jack. Settle down to work. Forget all those highfalutin ideals. Face the practical world. Come into our family business..."

"I'm sorry, Dad. I really am. But my ideals are important to me. They are my life. Without my ideals, I will be nothing. Dad, can't you see? I'm only being true to myself."

You turn to your annoyingly quiet wife for support: "Grace, help me! Why don't you say something? Talk some sense into him."

Grace does not know what to say. Then she has a sudden inspiration.

"Jack, why don't you go and have a chat with Father Goh. He's at St. Paul's now. He's always been a close friend to us. He'll know how to advise you, both you and Dad."

Father Goh calls to see you. He has had his talk with Jack.

"Well, Father, what do you think of all this talk about giving up on our family business? All this rubbish about going to work for the deaf?"

Father Goh looks at you with his frank and honest eyes. Those eyes of his have always been powerful weapons for the Lord's work.

"Joseph," he says, "do you know what I was reminded of when Jack talked to me about his ideals? I was reminded of a young man who once came to see me about becoming a priest."

You pause. He has stopped you in your tracks. He has hit you right between the eyes. "You mean?"

"Yes, I mean you. You have, of course, forgotten the conversations you had with me. You yourself, yes, you too, were once full of ideals. Full of dedication to the service of God and man. You thought only of a life given to your fellow human beings. Leading them to God."

"I was different then."

"As different as Jack is now."

You can think of no reply to this. Father Goh continues:

"Respect his stand, Joseph. Let him do what he believes in. He has to follow his own star. If you love him, let him go.

"He seems to be strong in his dedication to the handicapped. Let him fulfill, or at least dream out, his dream. You remember you could not fulfill your own dream? You recall how angry your own father was? And how, in the end, you had to give up your own ideals and follow him in his business?

"You were fed up then. Later you learned to accept your lot in life. And, in fact, you have done well. But have there not been moments when you've wondered whether you would not have been happier had you been given your own choice?"

You can only look at Father Goh's sincere face. You know he reads your heart. He has made a good point. You start to re-think. This is the beginning of your surrender.

And so you let your son Jack go back to London. You are reconciled. You give your blessing to his ideals. You subsidize him for his chosen course. Both materially and in spirit.

In the ensuing months you grow more and more to respect your son for his stand and his selfless aspiration. You place him on a pedestal. And you display him to all your friends. Almost as a saint.

Yes, you are proud of your son Jack. For following his star. For being true to himself. For his readiness to give up a life of ease and luxury to do work for the needy.

Indeed, although you do not say so, of course, you are also a little proud of yourself that, unlike your own obstinate father, you did not force your son to toe your line.

Your own idealism undergoes a revival. You give more to charity. You help to raise funds for good works. You even join visits to Homes and pay for treats for the underprivileged to Sentosa, Mandai Zoo and other places.

You and your wife also begin to attend church services and community service meetings more frequently. You both help in evangelical work. You are born again. To your religion, to your fellow-men—and to your ideals.

You have now reduced your workload. Sold your restaurant interests and invested in less time-consuming business. You and your wife now have more time away from pure money-making.

"Father Goh," you enthuse to the good priest one day, "Jack has really shown us the light. Both Grace and I have learned from his ideals. Jack is really a wonderful boy, isn't he? He'll finish and be home in a few months. It'll be great to have him back. When he left, he said he wanted to come back and join one of our handicapped schools here."

"Let's wait and see," Father Goh says cautiously. "Let's wait till he succeeds in his course. Let's see if he still wants the same thing."

You feel a tinge of unease. But you laugh it off.

You know your son Jack. He's a serious boy. And he sees through what he sets out to do. Didn't he even wait till he'd finished his Business Administration course before he sprang his completely new aspirations on you.

Yes, you know your Jack. He will succeed. After all the course takes only a year for postgraduates. It should be easy for him.

The year has passed quickly. Jack comes home again. As usual, he has not been writing frequently. And he communicates on the phone just as rarely. So you only get sporadic glimpses into his life in the UK—cryptic communications of little rapport and less import.

Yes, Jack comes home, complete with his Diploma in Education for the Handicapped. He seems to have grown older than should be for only one year.

The next day you ask him his plans.

"Dad," he says, focusing his open eyes on you. "I've something to say to you. Just don't be shocked. In the last year, I've got really close to handicapped work. I don't think I have what it takes. It calls for a lot of dedication. More than I can sustain.

"I've seen the dedicated ones. How they can take anything and carry on. I've also seen those who start off like myself. Ready and eager. But before long they find out they're not really cut out for such demanding work. But they still plod on. Soon it becomes too late to change. So they just carry on. Without the spirit they become uncaring robots. Or, worse still, angry and frustrated and lashing out without knowing why.

"I've also given a lot of thought to what you said last year about helping the handicapped in another way. By earning and donating to help the dedicated ones do their work. Your letters this past year show me how you really practice what you say."

You are too surprised to react. You just do not know what to say. After awhile your wife asks the question in both your minds:

"What do you plan to do, then?"

"Well, Mum," he answers, "there's this restaurant in London that's up for sale. Right at the end of Hope Street as it turns into Rich Lane. It's going reasonably cheap. And the takings are good. Probably makes a lot of money..."

Goh Sin Tub is a Singaporean who writes about Singaporeans. He has a wide spectrum of experience gained as a mechanic, teacher, civil servant, executive, banker, builder and social worker, and has a flair with words, both humorous and poignant. He is the Chairman of the Board of Governors of St. Joseph's Institution, his favorite charity.

"Simply understanding isn't enough, you have to act on what you understand!"

Showdown at Horton's

BY FAKIR BAYKURT

SOMEHOW or other the city of Duisburg had sunshine that day. White, black and gray pigeons bustled about the concrete, puttering, pecking, searching for something to eat.

Horton's big department store, its outside overlaid with decorations reminding one of honeycombs, was, using a very old Anatolian expression, only three steps from City Library. Streetcars passed between. Clanging, pre-war streetcars were no more. Present-day streetcars passed by silently with a "Jiiiizzzt!" The Metro system, underground, moved ahead in a form resembling mole tunnels.

The city, located where the Rhine and Ruhr Rivers meet, had grown; although ripped and torn in seven hundred places, like a black flower, it still grew. Children of immigrant workers from various European, Asian, and African countries scattered through its streets like swarms of flies. Workers' children, every color, race, and size, teemed in houses built a century ago in Hamborn, Meiderich, Hochfeld and Rheinhausen.

A century ago many migrant workers also came and worked in the mines, foundries, and blast furnaces. When Poles, French, and Italians of that time were able to move their wives and children from the louse-, flea-, and roach-infested barracks into these brick houses, they heaved deep sighs and said: "Hey, just look, really grand homes!" Now you couldn't get a dog to live there. They have shared toilets and no baths. It's cold two or three seasons of the year. Heat them if you can; coal heaters cost this much, electric heaters that much. Lots of them are sold at department stores, but even if you are able to get one after cutting expenses on this and that, they use current continually like water wheels on mills use water; each one burns up 1600 to 1700 marks in one winter.

Duisburg lives in crazy, strange, uncontrollable change. The city of a hundred years ago, with its narrow streets where one promenaded from one lovely neighborhood to the next, has long since vanished. Walsum and Dinslaken combined. Krefeld and Rahm combined. Now you enter one city without leaving the other. An automobile for one of every three people. Here Bochum, there Oberhausen, yonder Mülheim...Gelsenkirchen, Köln, Bonn close by on three- or four-lane, comfortable highways. On the road connecting Duisburg with Düsseldorf, one sees nothing but houses with flowered windows; it opens up only once to slope and countryside.

Anton Gebler, who works at the City Library, now denies it. "No, I'm not!" he says, but he came from last century's Polish miner, Patowsky's family. At that time too, foreign workers had no right to be employed in their own names, to establish towns, vote, be elected, or become citizens. For these reasons they discarded their own beautiful names, assumed German ones which they felt made them ladies and gentlemen to a degree, belched after eating lots of sausage and salami, and thought they could stand on their own two feet.

They weren't wrong. At one go Grandfather became a married man, took his *Gewerbe* and opened a store; in five or ten years, he converted the store to a department store, and refining his smattering of German a little, had even been able to become a government civil servant. Anton Gebler's grandfather considered his countrymen who were not Germanized backward. Now Anton, too, looks at these migrants from three continents just as his grandfather had at his own countrymen. He finds their appearance queer, their walking slow, their spitting in the streets uncouth, their staring at blonde women in streetcars ignorant, but their work at the job at the mines and foundries too fast and gets angry. He is very indignant at the ten to eighteen year old foreign workers' children's soiling the City Library reading room with their sunflower- and squash-seed hulls. When he goes into a rage, just like his grandfather of a century ago, he curses indecently. But new workers have improved their German swearing from day to day so Anton Gebler mutters most of his curses in a low voice because he is fearful as a mouse of becoming the subject of organized protests. Sometimes he swallows them back as if taking a cheap indigestion pill. At such times he crosses the streetcar tracks between City Library and Horton's and goes to see his high school classmate, Georg Bender.

Repair and construction work that began at the end of World War II is far from finished in the city. Large banks, insurance companies, business offices, and hotels were built. Tower-like, multi-level department stores, subways, elevated roads were opened. Still—biff bam, fast and noisy—construction and repair continues.

"Our lives are passing in babel and squalor!" grumbled Anton Gebler. Three days before, while following a television broadcast on the subject of environmental pollution, he put on his far-sighted glasses, and carefully examined a chart showing the world's dirtiest cities. While he noted Ankara, Chicago, and the names of I don't know how many other places, he was amazed he didn't come across the name of Duisburg, caught as it is between the chemical claws of Krupp, Thyssen, Mannesmann, and Bayer. His faith in God was shaken like his belief in the so-called poison of television. Next a chart of noisy cities appeared on the screen. He straightened his glasses and watched again. Still the name of this city, where living two years would put a person in the hospital, was missing. Hands in his pockets he quickly walked by Horton's brightly adorned show windows.

When he neared the store's main entrance, he ran into the heavy, lumbering bodies of two Turkish workers, Pazarcikli Ökkesh and Akyazili Ergün. Behind their backs, he suspected they smelled of onions and garlic. He slowed down to let them move on and make way, but there weren't only Turkish workers! Three German women, one holding a bulldog on leash, two wearing far-sighted glasses, holding plastic bags, and erect as if they'd swallowed walking sticks, were coming out. Hundreds of customers! Like a floating mine, Anton Gebler lunged into the crowd inside. Down the escalator, like a green, gravelly, muddied flood flowing down a streambed, poured Turkish women with head scarves, their skirts hanging over long print underpants. German girls who perhaps took an extra bath before going out, no longer wore brassieres. Mr. Gebler stood on a serrated escalator tread looking up and down in disgust. Hundreds of pre-war shops had been combined in one department store, constituting a business melting pot. The entry floor filled with a thousand products from underwear, shirts, sweaters to nylon raincoats, glasses, binoculars; from seven hundred kinds of candies to chocolates, picture frames to photographic equipment needs, from rouge, fingernail polish to belts; it looked like a seething picture he'd bought to frame a few days ago.

"It's seething, our city of 580,000 people! Its more than fifty thousand migrant workers, sprouts and all, sons, daughters, wives, children, are at a bubbling boil! My God, and they want the right to vote! Where should I go?"

He was completely enraged at the SPD's (Social Democratic Party) young spokesmen getting confused now and again and voting to give these people the right to vote. He finished the first floor and looked again at those riding the escalators from the second floor where Ready-to-wear, Women's, Men's, Summer, and Winter departments were located. Unimpressed, disgusted, he walked under electric lights that consumed a world of electricity, among shoppers turning over merchandise or buying and having things wrapped. Knocking as a joke, he entered the back room where his friend, Georg Bender, was sitting alone.

Georg Bender was in charge of inspection and control. He operated with closed circuit television equipment. Large and small thefts continually occurred in the store. The equipment where he sat was tied to twenty cameras. He switched this button on, that one off. Last winter he had found the opportunity to give his tall athletic body and wild womanizing heart a chance to rest in Wiesbaden. A few minutes before, he'd visited on the telephone with his new *kurshatten* (bathbunny or spasprite) he met there; they planned to get together again two weeks later...He switched the view to Books, a department he considered most sensitive and a little annoying.

At that moment, Pazarjikli Ökkesh and Akyazili Ergün arrived at the Book section where adventure novels were located on one side, expensive art books another, and travel guides, all of the same size, on yet another. Afyon Cream Hajer whom Pazarjikli Ökkesh had met and married here, was on leave in Turkey. Thank God the Istanbul office loan was about finished! He had received news that the shop for sale in Ankara was a steal. She'd gone to deposit a large portion of the money he'd squirreled away as a down payment. Hajer's plump sister, Sevim, was at work in the Old Folks Home.

Foxy Ökkesh had been going to one doctor then another for three months, and by wrapping Marash tobacco in his armpits, lying sick, and swallowing fresh olive pits, he feigned stomach ulcers and colitis in his intestines, thus wangling a long sick leave. He had completed ten years in Germany. In free time, while on sick leave from heavy labor at the Walsum kilns, he worked at a shop which sold meat, milk, and brooms to Moslems.

Ergün thought his brother-in-law a bigger goldbricker than necessary. He had finished six years, and realizing he couldn't talk properly with his poor German, quickly married a Turkish girl, Sevim. Like her name, Sevim was lovable, pretty, and also a rather progressive thinking, working girl. At strikes, at demonstration marches, Ergün promenaded his wife like a lily at his right side. Nights he read her books written about life's greatest passionate loves. The previous month he had deposited 1400 marks for enrollment in a condensed course; he had decided to improve his German. He was angry at himself for not doing this a long time ago. Turning it over in his Turkish head later he laughed, "In view of my coming so-o, so-o late, it means I'm one of the most dyed-in-the-wool Turks!"

Ökkesh saw how quickly his brother-in-law's German was

improving. From time to time he had fun saying, "Hey, come on! Talk a little *Hochdeutsch!*" Ökkesh not only had fun with Ergün, he told his comrades forty times a day in the Bachelor Workers Home how he fought in German with the *Meister* in his office the year they came, about his defiance in front of the Meister and from time to time, between his sentences, he enjoyed himself saying, I said, "*Ich!*" I said, "*Du!*" I said, "*Dich!*"

Ergün had an ache in his ankle. He intended to buy long underwear and flannel undershirts with sleeves. But Ökkesh said, "Come on!" and pulled him to the Book section. They paused briefly at expensive art books, then went on to the cheap novels. Ergün saw a copy of *Treasure Island* for five marks and bought it. He put the book in front of a girl with "Ulrike Weiser" pinned above her left breast. Ulrike Weiser put the money into the automatic register, bagged the book, and gave it to Ergün.

Ökkesh stood where he always stopped, in front of the shelves where various kinds of travel guides were arranged. Ergün came over, "Let's go to the Clothes section."

"At least have a little fun, brother-in-law; the Italians have put our books upside-down again!" He tried to find *Reiseführere Türkische* among the travel books which were all the same size. While doing that, he opened *Sardinia, Corsica,* and *Italy,* and scattered them about.

Georg Bender told Anton Gebler, "Come here, look!"

Anton's mind was on his approaching vacation and vacillating on the question of whether to go to the Canaries or Mediterranean Coast, so he didn't hear Georg's voice.

He repeated, "Look at what I'm going to show you!

His handsome swarthy face on the screen, Ökkesh converted his wrath to old curses. Wiping and polishing the 14.80 mark *Turkei* book's cover with the moon and crescent on it, he placed it on the top. *Spain, Bahamas, Athens, Peloponesia, Portugal,* whatever, he shoved underneath. After finding the 5.80 mark *Reiseführer Türkische* and placing it on top also, and comforted at having done a very important and heroic duty thousands of kilometers from the homeland, he followed his brother-in-law to the Underclothing section. In passing, he patted a child who was crying in Turkish, "Anaaa! Anaaa!" "Hush! Your mother's coming right away! Stay right here!" he said. He'd agreed with Afyon Cream Hajer. Three years later they would make a baby.

Pressing another button, Georg Bender followed Ökkesh and Ergün, but in the big crowd their images slowly got lost, so he gave up.

"Shall we have a cup of coffee?"

"*Ja,* let's. *Danke!*"

Secretary Monica made the coffee. Georg Bender leaned to the intercom and ordered two coffees.

The surveillance image was focused again on the Book section. At that point Moroccan El Mehdi, who worked with the city cleaning crew, came on the screen. He put the 5.80 *Morocco* which had fallen underneath, beside *Turkei.* Behind him, Spaniard Jose, who worked at meat cutting in Meiderich, took the 5.80 *Spain* from underneath and placed it on top, carefully pushing the others underneath.

"Did you see that?" Georg Bender laughed with pleasure. "This has been going on for a month! They never get tired of it!"

At that point Yugoslav Smaylagich came, took the 8.90 *Jugoslawiesche Küste und Inseln* and put it on top of the others.

"Every day the books go top or bottom a number of times. Can you imagine? Some go down, some come up. They all try to put their own country's book on top."

Italian construction worker Juvoni entered the screen now. In anger he narrowed his eyes, shadowed by black eyebrows, and looked. If he'd been in his own country, he'd have filled anyone who made him this angry full of holes. But in Germany the police were savage. Aah, beautiful *Sardinia, Sicily, Corsica,* and *Italy* had been put lower down, and odds and ends set up on top.

Anton Gebler caught the humor in the story developing on the screen, and laughed, "*Ach so!*" For awhile he babbled away like he was tied to a bobbin. "Bravo to our new guests!" he said rocking in his chair. Crossing one leg over the other, he belched sausage and salami. "There are all kinds of people in the world!" Lethargically he added, "Lots of cattle too, naturally."

Before Italian construction worker Juvoni left, Greek foundry worker Kosta arrived at the Book section. Searching for and finding *Mittelqriecheland* he placed it on top. Juvoni reached out his hand and prevented him from pushing his own books to the bottom.

At that point, Ökkesh carrying his bag of underwear he'd purchased, followed by Ergün, approached the travel guide table. "Hey, what kind of sly business is this?" Ökkesh yelled. As his brother-in-law was beside him, he exploded a curse in German and Turkish. "Uncircumcised bastards! I just corrected these a little while ago. Are you standing guard here? Don't touch! Just leave the books alone!" Leaning a little he found the 14.80 M. *Turkei* and 5.80 M. *Reiseführer Türkische* and again placed them on top.

Juvoni saw the Turks were two, he was one. He looked for the possibility of support, but Kosta stood quietly at the other end of the table. He didn't want a fight. His books hadn't dropped far down anyway.

"And what kind of smart trick is this? We'll take care of it!" said Ökkesh. In order to give books concerning Turkey better exposure, he lowered books both Juvoni and Kosta had put on top to the bottom.

Spanish Jose appeared on the other side and stopped two paces from the table. He saw the books he'd put on top lowered and let out a "Tüüüh!" Even if Greek Kosta backed him, he had no hope of support from Juvoni because he didn't like Italians. He stopped where he was.

Moroccan El Mehdi, who had bought four "Camels" and something to eat, came up from the first floor. He walked like a benevolent desert lizard. Showing his pearly teeth he greeted the Turks in his smattering of German. He understood both the situation and those who had come to the books. In front of him Ökkesh moved the 5.80 M. *Marokko* to a position on top. They looked at each other voluntarily. El Mehdi stood beside Ökkesh and smiled a little more with his white teeth. Then Juvoni and Kosta slid together as if moved by magnets. It was three against three.

Upstairs, Anton Gebler let out another laugh: "God, this is theater! *Kleiner Mann was tun?*" (Little man doesn't seem to know what to do!) He sipped his coffee, slurp-slurp. "I think the Canary Islands are worn out, slurp. Let's go together to the Dalmatian Coast, slurp. I know a tour, slurp. Three weeks, including breakfast 550 marks a person, slurp. We'll economize on food at grills, slurp.

Georg Bender sensed that the toughening argument in the Book section was about to turn into a fight. "New festival plays seem to begin in our department store!" he said. At that moment, Yugoslav Smaylagich entered the screen. Ergün wasn't for raising a rumpus, but he couldn't allow his own brother-in-law to be mistreated right before his eyes. He looked suspiciously at Smaylagich. It was obvious from his type that he was Yugoslav. But I wonder whose side he would take? This depended on whether or not he was Moslem. How would he know that? In his rather advanced German and in order to change the talk around a bit, he asked, "All the infidels support each other! But I wonder when we Moslems will wake up?"

Smaylagich looked, *Jugoslawiesche Küste und Inseln* had gone way down, wasn't even visible. He slipped up to the table and started to hurriedly search. Ergün saw the book before he did, and with shrewd thinking put it between *Turkei* and *Marokko*. He looked at the threesome, Kosta, Juvoni, and Jose standing there: "Gentlemen," he said, "if you don't want some kind of trouble, you better take off!"

Greek Kosta mellowed, saying, "But we're neighbors! Please, if we put yours side-by-side with ours?"

"Come on now, you can't fool us!" said Ökkesh waving the back of his hand toward Kosta. "You know you'll take a beating so you're toadying with this neighbor stuff! That's not what you say on television every now and then!" He pushed Kosta in the chest.

Then Juvoni pushed Ökkesh. Jose moved. He raised his clenched butcher's fist. He was going to hit Ökkesh in the neck, Moroccan El Mehdi caught the fist in the air and turned it back into Jose's face.

It was a showdown.

"You'll never believe it, Anton. There's very bad business going on below!" Georg Bender said and leaned over the intercom: "Electrician Hans! Electrician Hans! Foreigners are starting a disturbance on the entrance floor! Quick! Hurry to the Book Department! Sales clerk Elvira! Sales clerk Elvira! Floor security man Jacobi! Go to the Book Department, please!"

Electrician Hans arrived at the scene immedately.

Fluttering out of breath, Elvira was about to jump in between them. Security man Jacobi yelled, "Sto-op Bayoghlu Baylar!"

Customers gathered around. District policemen, Günter Brodkorb and Hubert Huck arrived. Georg Bender also came down from upstairs. Ökkesh and El Mehdi must have found all this pushing and crowding disgraceful, so they laid one each on Jose and Kosta. Juvoni found his chance and laid one on Ökkesh, blacking his left eye like an opium poppy. Ökkesh, surprised momentarily by the blow, let go with a swift kick. The toe of his Italian shoe (which he'd bought a year ago because they were so durable) missed Juvoni where he aimed and hit Electrician Hans's knee, bruising it. Hubert Huck jumped in and grabbed Ökkesh by the neck. Günter Brodkorb blew his whistle. Sales clerk Elvira cried, "We've run into trouble! My God! Why all this from these foreigners?"

Georg Bender said, "Listen to me, gentlemen!" and coughed. Actually, he was about to give a speech. Sales clerk Elvira pursed her lips, she well knew the old lecher's character.

Policeman Huck interrupted, "More important you listen to us Mr. Bender! We've got to pick these people up right now and take them to the station!"

"No! Let them listen to me for a few minutes! Maybe we can solve the problem here! Then it won't be necessary to go to the station! For over a month children's theater has been playing here! All of our new "guests" first come here, one by one. They take the travel books pertaining to their country and place them on top, then the others put them on the bottom. I see it clearly from upstairs. Today they all met."

Policeman Huck shouted, "*Ach so*! I've probably found the solution!" and laughed. "Why don't you line the books up side by side on a shelf instead of one on top of the other. Leave the books in one row, all next to each other."

Georg Bender: "No, that's impossible! The book table will not be changed! Our guests must change their minds."

Policeman Brodkorb's eyes grew large: "You consider this possible, my dear sir? After all, their heads aren't detachable! You can't take one off and put another on!"

"No, my dear policeman, not with that meaning!"

Anton Gebler was alone upstairs. He saw his high school friend giving a speech to the migrant workers. Policeman Huck thought of quickly dispersing the crowd that had gathered. As for Georg Bender, he continued his ponderous speech word by word. The crowd, composed of more migrant workers than Germans, had to listen to his speech to the very end.

"Look, this is a big department store. There's a world of capital invested here! We've assembled hundreds of people here to serve you. We have formed a beautiful institution of commerce in the center of the city. You live in a civilized country, in a great city. Be careful of your behavior. Show respect and understanding for each other's value. You can't achieve progress by coming to the books from morning till night and putting one on top, another on the bottom! Do you understand what I'm saying, gentlemen? It's easy to put the books on top, or bottom every day! The thing that's difficult, important, and necessary is to elevate your "land" to put it on top. Do you understand what I'm saying?"

I wonder what this jughead's saying, thought Spaniard Jose.

Moroccan El Mehdi: "I'm not powerful enough to raise a gigantic 'land' and put it on top of Italy or Greece. Even if I were, I can't cross the Mediterranean, it would pour, scatter apart, God forbid!"

Ökkesh thought of what he'd learned in the Pazarcik middle school: My country is high anyway! Mount Ararat 5165 meters, Erciyas 3916, Hasan 3258.

Georg Bender transferred the weight of his slightly overweight body from right to left foot. The migrant workers standing in the middle of the assembled crowd like criminals, muttered, "Let's not go to the station, no harm, we'll listen to a little speech!" Whether they could understand it or not, they could endure this much talk.

"It's necessary to work hard and progress, gentlemen! Understand well what I say! Simply understanding isn't enough, you have to act on what you understand! Now I request that for this once the respected police not take you to the station! All right?"

Policeman Huck looked at his comrade. In his goose-dropping-green eyes he could read nothing but a mixture of fear mixed with respect he felt for the authority of Horton's Department Store, more than half of whose capital came from big American companies. But there had been very serious shoving and fisticuffs, Electrician Han's knee had even been bruised by a kick. Furthermore, the customers had gathered and were watching. He didn't know what to do. It would be a good idea to go to the car and ask the chief by radio.

At that moment, blessedly, Electrician Hans came to his rescue: "It's not important, officer! The bruise on my knee will be gone in a week. Just go about your business." Internal security chief Georg Bender had influence in any case.

"Then off with you!" said Policeman Huck.

Ökkesh, El Mehdi, Juvoni, Kosta, and Smaylagich had no trouble understanding, "Off with you!" They relaxed for an instant. But it didn't last long. Realizing the recording on closed television would be seen as a record of their past offenses, they closed ranks. Drawing back with their eyes as if nailed to the eyes of the police, they left the scene of the incident. The police seemed like rabbits or lambs anyway.

Outside, the noisy life of the city poured along from past to future, its blue and green faded like the Rhine, like the Rhine which meets the Ruhr at this place. The sun had withdrawn behind thick chemical clouds. Ökkesh walked along rubbing the black eye on the left of his handsome swarthy face muttering, "Mount Süphan 4434, Alagöz Mountain 4094, Allahüekber 3111."

Suddenly, "Did that jughead say bad things to us, brother-in-law?" he asked Ergün. Passing the Union Bank and City Library they came to the streetcar stop. "You spent a month's pay on that *Hochdeutsch* course. Now tell me what that fatso said. By God, I'm really mad about what happened today!"

Grinning, Ergün nodded his head forward and back: "The German talked in paragraphs, like a book!"

"He raised and lowered 'lands' didn't he?"

Ergün didn't want his brother-in-law to think the German he'd spent all that money to learn was weak, so he started translating at length what Georg Bender said, together with what he hadn't said. "Lion brother-in-law, when he told us, 'Raise your land,' he didn't mean put land on top of land, he meant to say: raise the economy, the commerce, but not by raising and lowering the books. Pucker your ass and raise your country!

he said, you understand? It's necessary to progress in production and management! he said. Otherwise you came to earth as a suckling calf and you'll go as an ox; but whatever—coming or going—you won't know crap! he said. Leave off hitting each other in the face with your fists and disgracing yourselves, or next time I'll turn you all over to the *Ausländer Polizei*! Upstairs I took your pictures. You do this again and I'll immediately ship you back to your countries across the border! he said. You understand?"

"I understand, tiger brother-in-law," said Ökkesh.

Ergün stretched out the translation until the streetcar stop to their home in Meiderich, where houses looked as though built under Thyssen smoke a century ago.

"I understand, crazy brother-in-law."

Streetcar number 904 would soon come. But before it came, Greek foundry worker Kosta appeared at the stop. When he saw Ergün and Ökkesh, eyes on the ground, he was about to laugh. Behind him appeared Italian Juvoni. He walked up slowly. Like Germans greet each other morning, noon, and night, he tossed in a cynical, cold, "Guten Tag!" Ökkesh remained silent. Ergün simply moved his lips: "Guten Tag!"

Before long, Spanish Jose and Moroccan El Mehdi arrived, one standing at one end of the stop, one at the other. Soon, Yugoslav Smaylagich appeared.

Then the Meiderich streetcar came.

They packed the vehicle without pushing or shoving each other. Slowly gaining speed over rails laid after the war, they flowed along.

Around the streetcar stop, white, black and gray pigeons were still looking for something to eat.

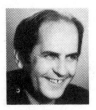

Born in 1929, in Akcha, Fakir Baykurt has become one of Turkey's great short story writers and novelists. He specializes in social comment about Turkey's villages and peasants. His translator, Joseph S. Jacobson, is a university professor who has translated several Turkish stories for scholarly journals.

"Unfortunately, our differences again rose to the surface almost as soon as we arrived in Jiddah."

Feast of Love

BY TODD ROLF ZEISS

THERE are some posts where one feels immediately at home, others that seem a bit strange but, eventually, one adjusts. Occasionally, however, one takes a post at which one never feels comfortable. My stay in T'aif, Saudi Arabia, was one of those.

It shouldn't have been. I had been invited by Akmed bin Saluwi, a prince through marriage to the House of Saud and one of the richest Arabs in the region. The invitation had been extended by the prince's son, Khalid, my roommate and *little brother* at Dartmouth.

"Come home with me, Samuel," he said, having at last graduated after interrupting his college career for three years to serve as an official observer for his uncle, King Faisel, at the United Nations. (I doubt the interruption was unwelcomed.) "With your wisdom and my father's money," Khalid continued, "we will build a beautiful city together, one with grand villas and fountains and shrubberies and..."

"...a racetrack?" I jabbed, knowing Khalid's fondness for fine horse flesh.

"Of course," he replied, exuberantly. "How else are we to enjoy the sport of kings?"

That his father could afford such a city was hardly an issue. Since the establishment of the Arabian-American Oil Company and, later, OPEC, money had been pouring into that relatively small kingdom almost as fast as the royal family could find ways to spend it, and even the strictures placed on them by King Faisel did little to curb their extravagance.

Indeed, while in school, Khalid raced around in a Jaguar roadster and would dash down to New York City with every change of season to buy himself a new wardrobe. Initially, upon his return, he offered his old wardrobe to me.

"No thanks," I replied. "Give them to someone who truly needs them."

"But they are fine clothes, excellent clothes, made by the best of tailors," he cried, unable to fathom my simpler ways.

"All the more reason to give them to someone else," I replied.

At first he thought me a consummate snob, unwilling to wear cloth that had touched another's flesh, and this infuriated him. Then he thought he had insulted me, demeaned my status by offering me his castaways, and as a result grew so abject that he feared even to speak to me. Finally he came to understand that I felt comfortable in my slacks, tweed and gabardine jackets and open, button-down collars and would feel anything but in three-piece, pin-striped suits, starched collars and French cuffs. We became friends once again, and very close friends when at last he understood that I didn't in any way hold him in contempt for the manner in which he chose to dress.

But that had been seven years ago. Khalid was now a Dartmouth graduate and I, in the meantime, had completed an advanced degree in municipal planning, spent two years in Gabon with the Peace Corps and another in the Sudan with the American Friends' Service Committee. Yet none of my activities in those two countries lay in what I was trained to do—plan cities. So when Khalid extended the invitation, I accepted without giving it a second thought.

Unfortunately, our differences again rose to the surface almost as soon as we arrived in Jiddah. We were whisked from the airport in a Mercedes limousine bearing the prince's flags on its front fenders and preceded by a Mercedes sedan carrying four bodyguards who made a great show of their pistols and submachine guns. Following us was another Mercedes sedan carrying Khalid's and my luggage, his two manservants and their luggage, and two more bodyguards, equally proud of their weaponry. Upon leaving the airport grounds, the three cars accelerated rapidly, weaving in and out of traffic, first on one side of the road, then on the other, narrowly missing cars, trucks, carts and pedestrians, our three drivers operating, apparently, under the illusion that merely by blowing their horns they created an instant right of way.

"Can we go a bit more slowly?" I asked.

Khalid glared at me as if I had violated the most sacred of trusts.

"There is no need," he said, coolly.

We quickly left the city and its traffic and raced across open desert which, unfortunately, presented another hazard—drifting sand. As the car ahead of us flew through the small drifts that lay across the roadway, it kicked up a veritable storm of dust and flying sand which obscured our vision and spattered against the limousine with a sound like sleety rain. *How can they drive through stuff like this and keep these cars so shiny?* I asked myself, seeing in my mind's eye the brightwork and finish being sandblasted away. Then I realized that my mind and values were stuck back in the mid-sixties, waxing and polishing the '49 Plymouth coupe handed down to me by my father. We were now in the late seventies, and if one of Prince Akmed's Mercedes grew dull, he simply bought a new one.

At the speeds we were traveling, it was not long before we passed the outskirts of Mecca and turned onto the winding road to T'aif. In spite of its chuckholes, blind curves and neck-snapping switchbacks, we rapidly climbed the escarpment east of the Plain of Arafat and were soon on the outskirts of T'aif.

With a loud blast of the horn and a screeching of tires, our limousine suddenly careened to the left, then back to the right, and I had just enough time to catch a glimpse of a bus, its hood thrown up and its engine burning, having collided, apparently, with a truck that rested half-on and half-off the roadway a few yards beyond. I thought I saw several bodies lying on the pavement.

"Shouldn't we stop?" I asked. "They may need help!"

"No, no," said Khalid, obviously unconcerned. "There are those who take care of such things."

My meeting with Prince Akmed the following day proved no more favorable. He made it clear to me that he was perfectly happy with the spontaneous and disorderly development of T'aif and wanted no foreign infidel mucking it up. If, however, Khalid and I insisted on laying out a city, we could work on R'abad, thirty miles to the southeast, where he planned to build another palace, a sort of hideaway from the pressures in T'aif. We could have a free hand so long as the palace faced Mecca and had a four-lane highway running straight to it.

Though I had some trepidations about the latter, I was eager to get to work and urged Khalid to take me to R'abad at once.

"First there is someone I want you to meet," he said, his eyes sparkling.

Once more we climbed into the prince's limousine—this time with only the driver and one bodyguard—and we were whisked to an estate near the edge of the city. On the way we again passed the wrecked bus. Its hood was still up but the fire was out. Not far from it rested the hapless truck in exactly the same position it had been the day before. And there were bodies, three of them—all quite bloated, one lying in a pool of blackened blood.

I looked at Khalid. He pressed the button that lowered the glass partition between us and the driver and bodyguard, gave a quiet but firm order, then raised the partition once again.

"It will be taken care of," he said.

The estate was a rather grand place with a large house and a high stone wall surrounding the immediate grounds, and I was certain we were going to meet an important friend or, perhaps, Khalid's fiancée, for I had learned when we were roommates in college that he had been betrothed at age fourteen. I was rather surprised, therefore, when we drove past the house and down a long, straight drive to the stables. No sooner had we stepped from the car when a groom appeared, leading a handsome, dappled Arabian stallion.

"Isn't he beautiful!" exclaimed Khalid.

"Marvelous," I replied, walking about the spirited animal who pranced sideways, eyeing me with suspicion. "Where in the world did you find him?"

Khalid smiled broadly. "He is of my own breeding," he said, with unabashed pride. "I call him Ibn al-Reigh, Son of the Wind. With him I am going to win the Race of Princes. It is still two months away and already he outruns last year's winner." Looking at the superb animal, I had no reason to doubt either of Khalid's declarations. "Would you like to see him run?" he asked.

"Yes," I replied. "Yes, indeed."

A few moments later, Khalid's driver, his bodyguard and I stood at the rail of a practice track to the rear of the stone wall as the groom led Son of the Wind, now under saddle, out onto the track, with Khalid, wearing jodphurs and riding boots, aboard.

With a piercing *Hi-yeeeee*, Khalid spurred the animal. Son of the Wind lunged forward and was soon rounding the first turn. As he rounded the second turn and moved along the far rail, I caught a true sense of his amazing speed. He seemed to fly, to float, his neck stretching forward and back, his legs a blur beneath him. He rounded the third turn, then the fourth, and came thundering down the stretch, moving smoothly, easily, yet with incredible speed, Khalid hovering over his withers, seeming to float, too, with only his arms moving in easy rhythm with the horse's stride.

"What do you say now, Samuel?" Khalid called, after turning the horse and bringing him up at an easy canter. "Surely I shall win, *in sh'allah!*"

"*In sh'allah,*" I said, giving the phrase an inflection which emphasized its conditional nature—"*If* God wills it."

"Ah, Samuel," Khalid laughed, "always the catechist. But there is another saying: 'That which can be, will be; and that which will be, is the will of Allah.' And it will be that I shall win the Race of Princes."

"We, too, have a saying," I replied, "and that is: 'Don't count your chickens before they hatch.'"

We left Son of the Wind with his groom, returned to the car, and were whisked back to T'aif. As we passed the spot where the collision had occurred, I noted that both the truck and the bus had been removed. The bodies, too, were gone, and all that remained was a large, black spot of dried blood on the pavement.

The following day Khalid and I were driven southeast toward R'abad. Once beyond the limits of T'aif, the road quickly deteriorated to little more than a winding track strewn with rocks and monstrous chuckholes, neither of which deterred our driver who raced along at frightening speed, blowing his horn and swerving around heavily laden donkeys, pedestrians and, occasionally, other vehicles. After well over an hour of his hair-raising maneuvers, we arrived at an oasis around which were scattered in no particular order a dozen or so mud houses.

"This is it?" I asked, stepping from the limousine.

Khalid smiled, "R'abad," he said.

"But there's nothing here!" I protested.

"Consider it—how do the French say? *Carte blanche*," he replied.

I shot him a nasty look, then walked quickly toward a low out-cropping of rock a hundred yards away. Climbing it, I surveyed the area, noting that the houses, which at first seemed randomly scattered, were situated along the banks of a *wadi*, an underground stream, and that the oasis lay in a rather deep natural bowl and was undoubtedly fed by the *wadi*. I climbed down from the out-cropping and, as I hiked about the area, roughly pacing off distances, my mind began to sketch various possibilities for the layout of the city. So absorbed was I in my preliminary calculations that it was not until I was nearly back to the limousine that I saw it was surrounded by a group of Arabs shaking their fists and all shouting at once. In their midst stood Khalid and his bodyguard, shouting and gesturing with equal ferocity. Only Khalid's driver, who sat in the air-conditioned limousine calmly smoking a cigarette, remained above the fray.

"What's all the ruckus about?" I asked, elbowing my way

through the crowd to Khalid's side.

"These stupid *Nadjis*," Khalid spat, "don't want our city. They want us to go away and leave them to live in the stink of their goats' dung."

I was not particularly surprised by the vociferousness of Khalid's statement, given his mercurial temperament. He was a member of the *Hijazi*, the more cosmopolitan coastal tribesmen, and was related to the House of Saud only by marriage. The roots of the royal house lay among the *Nadji*, the conservative inland tribes who believed themselves the only *true* Arabs and were highly suspicious of all outside influences.

"And what did you tell them?" I asked.

"I told them we would build the city anyway, and if they didn't like it they could clear out."

For a moment I felt as if I'd been transported to Hollywood and was playing a role in a *B* Western. At the same instant, there echoed in my ears the Arab saying, "I and my brother against my cousin; I and my cousin against the world," reminding me of the ancient Arab proclivity for disputation.

"Tell them," I said, drawing as deeply as I could upon my own heritage for settling disputes, "that if we build the city—and stress the word *if*—we will not displace anyone, and everyone will have a house with electric lights and water running inside."

Khalid translated my words. The crowd murmured among itself, gesturing emphatically. Then one man, whose name I later learned was Ahmed al-Kabir, stepped forward and asked Khalid several questions.

"He wants to know if his house will have a sunken bathtub," Khalid translated, "and if there will be flushing toilets."

"If that's what he wishes, yes."

"And a telephone?"

"Only for speaking the words of the Prophet and other important messages," I responded.

Again Khalid translated and again the crowd murmured and gestured, this time smiling and nodding their heads in approval. Again al-Kabir spoke.

"He wants to know where the palace will be built," said Khalid.

"Tell him I've not yet decided."

No sooner had Khalid translated my words than there came an angry buzzing from the crowd.

"But tell them," I said, raising my voice to be heard, "that if they choose three men as a council, when I complete my plans I shall present them for their approval, and that we will not do anything until we reach consensus."

Once more Khalid translated, and as he spoke the word *ijma* (meaning consensus, understanding and, in certain contexts, wisdom), the crowd again broke into smiles, nodding vigorously and murmuring expressions of satisfaction and pleasure.

When we reported our negotiations to Prince Akmed that evening, he was not at all pleased with having his desires subject to the approval of those he considered little better than unwashed rabble. Nor was Khalid especially happy with me, for I had, in a sense, forced him, a *Hijaz*, to eat his words before a group of despised *Nadjis*. Nevertheless, I plunged into the task of designing the city, spending the better part of a month surveying and plotting the entire area and making rough sketches of my plans. Often I was followed about by several of the boys of R'abad, and I hired two or three each day to carry my water and my portfolio, and even trained a couple of the older boys to handle my survey poles, for which Khalid's driver was extremely grateful. Having found the work too hot and tiring and beneath his dignity, he preferred to sit in the air-conditioned limousine, smoke cigarettes, and read forbidden pornographic magazines.

I took very quickly to wearing Arab garb and found their loose, flowing garments far cooler and more comfortable than Western collared shirts, belted trousers and tightly tied shoes, and I quickly fell into the habit of eating a light lunch of fruit and tea beneath the shade of the date palms along the margin of the oasis during the heat of the day. Whenever a villager showed an interest in what I was doing, I freely opened my portfolio and expressed as best I could in broken Arabic what I had in mind. These impromptu meetings soon became informal noonday sessions with a great deal of chattering, nodding and pointing as my plan slowly became clear. They were quite pleased with the way in which I had transformed the Prince's requirement of a four-lane highway into a lovely boulevard with a sprinkler system to water palms and low-growing shrubbery and, to my surprise, were delighted with the race track I had planned for the edge of the city, for the *Nadji* are, themselves, great horsemen. Then one day the three elders of the village who had been elected as the approving body came to me and complained sorrowfully that I was undercutting their authority.

"You tell everyone everything," wailed their spokesman, Ahmed al-Kabir. "You leave nothing for *us* to decide."

After apologizing profusely, I explained to them in broken Arabic that I was a stranger in their country and was, perhaps, overly solicitous for fear of giving offense. Nonetheless, I assured them, they would have the final say over what was and what was not to be done.

Unfortunately, I had spoken too soon.

Prince Akmed, by the power of the almighty purse, had the final word, and he spoke it by saying nothing. Always rather aloof, he had never given me a chance to get to know him and *vice versa*, and since King Faisel had ordered a crackdown on the spendthrift habits of the royal family, Prince Akmed found the village of R'abad rather convenient to forget. Then, too, my presence in T'aif was due primarily to the influence of his son, and with Khalid off training Son of the Wind, my importance within the household waned rapidly. Indeed, even Khalid's driver now deigned to make me wait for him.

The only bright moment during those dismal weeks came when Khalid, true to his word, won the Race of Princes.

He was ecstatic, absolutely jubilant. Like a small boy, he could not sit still when speaking of the event—and he spoke of it incessantly. Nor was his delight an empty one, for he immediately picked up a retinue of lesser princelings who went everywhere with him, admiring him, praising him, and speaking of nothing else but horse racing and Khalid's grand victory. Whenever I spoke about R'abad, or of urging his father to procure the heavy machinery required to lay the terrain, he shrugged me off, saying, "All in good time, my friend. It is bad manners to pressure a prince. It will be done, *in sh'allah*."

Unfortunately, without my knowledge, pressure was building in another quarter. The citizens of R'abad, now eager to have their town transformed into a beautiful city, were also chafing at the delay. Being *Nadjis* and far more egalitarian than the *Hijazis*, they sent Ahmed al-Kabir and the council of elders to Riad, where they demanded an audience with King Faisel. The king sent for Khalid's father, and very quickly the matter blew into a royal brouhaha that lasted for weeks, with each side claiming both innocence and injury.

It seemed obvious to me that nothing would get done and that I was wasting my time remaining in T'aif, so I turned my portfolio of elevations, projections and drawings over to Khalid, booked a seat on the next flight from Jiddah to Rome, and began packing my things.

I was still packing when Khalid burst into my apartment.

"It has been settled," he cried. "My little brother is going to marry the daughter of Ahmed al-Kabir, and we are going to have a great feast to celebrate their betrothal. You are to be the guest of honor."

I stood, a pair of socks in one hand, my razor in the other, speechless.

"You will come, of course," Khalid pressed.

"What about R'abad?" I asked. "Will it be built?"

"In good time," Khalid replied, prevaricating. "*In sh'allah*."

I returned to my packing.

"You must come," Khalid pleaded. "Ahmed al-Kabir insists. You have become known as a man of *ijma*, and it is important that you sit between him and my father and that you bless the betrothal."

"If I come," I said, turning to face Khalid, "will you promise to bend every effort toward the building of R'abad?"

Khalid looked away. "I promise," he said.

"Have I your word of honor as a prince of the House of Saud?"

Still not looking at me, he replied, "You have my word."

The feast was held in a long pavillion set up on the escarpment midway between T'aif and R'abad. As the guests, all men dressed in traditional Arab costume complete with ceremonial daggers, entered, they presented gifts to Khalid's father and to Ahmed al-Kabir and were greeted by them with the customary embrace and kiss. To my surprise, some of the Nadjis had even brought gifts for me, embracing me warmly, as if I were the prodigal son returned. They then filed down the pavillion and seated themselves on the carpets and cushions scattered in profusion over the sand—Prince Akmed's family on one side, al-Kabir's on the other.

The banquet opened with a speech by al-Kabir, welcoming the Hijazis and expressing his delight in the betrothal of his daughter to Kahlid's brother, whom he praised highly. Prince Akmed then welcomed the Nadjis, praising al-Kabir's daughter and declaring his joy over the pending marriage. They then turned to me and I suddenly realized that I, too, was expected to speak.

"Let us seek the blessing of Allah," I said and bowed my head in silent prayer, my mind whirling, damning Khalid, on the one hand, for not having warned me so I could have been prepared, and trying to figure out, on the other, exactly what I should and should not say. To my immediate relief, I gathered from the whispering I heard nearby that the assembly was quite impressed with the man of ijma who could speak directly to Allah without moving his lips or uttering a sound.

I then praised the betrothal as signifying the strengthening of the union between the two great peoples of Saudi Arabia.

"In token of this union," I said, "I am pleased to announce the following gifts: the people of R'abad present to Prince Akmed bin Jaluwi three-and-a-half acres of land adjacent to the never-failing spring in R'abad upon which to build his grand palace, plus sufficient right-of-way for a four-lane boulevard leading to it."

This was already in the plans approved by the Nadji council and, since he had dominion over but owned no land in R'abad, it was a great concession to the prince. There immediately came from the Hijazi side a great hubbub of discussion, and the prince himself smiled broadly. The Nadjis, stunned at first, quickly realized what a coup this could prove—for if the prince owned land in R'abad, surely he would build the city—and they, too, began to smile.

"And in response to this glorious gift," I declared, raising my voice over the hubbub, which immediately ceased, "and knowing what fine horsemen and lovers of fine horses the *Nadjis* are, with full consent of his son Khalid, Prince Akmed bin Suluwi grants to Ahmed al-Kabir and the citizens of R'abad the exclusive rights to the seed of Son of the Wind."

There came from the *Nadji* side an outburst of cheers and bright ululations. Khalid glared at me. I smiled back at him and nodded toward his father, who was smiling broadly and nodding again and again to accept the many compliments being paid him. Khalid looked about him, shrugged, then also smiled.

At this point the Arab band hired to entertain us began to play as tray after tray of roast lamb, locusts, dates, figs, rice cakes and other delicacies were brought in. Everyone fell noisily to eating. From time to time, compliments were shouted up to the prince and al-Kabir, who acknowledged them with gracious nods.

All seemed to be going splendidly; I was congratulating myself on having at last understood the Arab mentality when, at the far end of the pavillion, an argument broke out and raced like wildfire up the two rows of guests. Soon everyone was shouting at everyone else and food and drinking cups were flying through the air from one side of the pavillion to the other. Suddenly a *Hijazi* leaped to his feet and shook his fist in the face of a *Nadji*, who jumped up and did the same.

I was appalled. How long, I wondered, before they put their ceremonial daggers to unceremonious use? Frightened by the thought, I stood up, looking for the nearest exit.

Prince Akmed and al-Kabir also rose, each shouting at his constituency something about offending the man of *ijma* and dishonoring their respective houses.

Almost as quickly as it had begun, the dispute subsided. Prince Akmed and al-Kabir sat down.

"Sit, please," said the prince, tugging at the cuff of my trousers. "Sit and finish your meal. Please!"

I resumed my seat; the band began to play again; more food was brought out, and the banquet continued as before.

The following day I was surprised to learn from Khalid that his father and brother had gone on a trip to London and Paris to purchase goods for the wedding.

"When will they be back?" I asked.

"Who knows?" Khalid shrugged. "In a month or two, maybe three."

"Did he leave any instructions about R'abad?"

With apparent unconcern, Khalid shook his head

"Take me to the airport at Jiddah," I said, my patience totally exhausted.

As I was about to board my flight, Khalid said, "When my father returns you must come back and we will build our city."

I smiled but said nothing.

"We will," he said. "I promise."

I turned and started up the ramp.

"I promise you, Samuel," Khalid called, "It will be built. It is the will of God that it be so. You will come back, won't you?"

"*In sh'allah*," I called and, without breaking stride, continued up the ramp.

 *Todd Rolf Zeiss was born in North Dakota on February 13, 1936, a day when the temperature was minus 53 degrees. His physician father delivered him, went out on a house call, got caught in a blizzard, and wasn't seen for three days. That's a story Mr. Zeiss had plans to write about. Social, jovial, and musically talented, he has raced sports cars, shown dogs and taught imaginative writing and aesthetics on the university level. He has won prizes for both his poetry and short stories. His work has been published throughout the USA and Great Britain. His story "At the Post Office" appeared in SSI No. 46.*

"The only difficulty was in not appearing too
available to the socially ambitious and
thus watering their stock-in-trade."

Charity, Goddess of
Our Day

BY LOUIS AUCHINCLOSS

MYRON Townsend believed that his life, or at least the better part
of it, had ended on the winter afternoon in 1985 when, in a fit of
anger and humiliation, he had flung his resignation from the firm
of Townsend, Cox & Collins in the face of the managing partner,
Ralph Collins. He had not been obliged to do so. He had survived,
technically speaking, what was odiously known in Manhattan legal
circles as a "partnership purge." But the price would have been to
become a figurehead at a fixed stipend that was slightly less than
what the firm paid a first-year law clerk.

Myron, passing through the reception hall on his way home that
night and paying what he thought might be his farewell to the
three portraits hanging there, wondered grimly whether they did
not mark the stages of the decline and fall of the Townsends. His
own clear recognition of that seemingly ineluctable process added
the final drop to the brew of his bitterness. The large dark canvas
that depicted his grandfather Sidney, the firm founder, by Daniel

Huntington showed a corpulent gentleman in a Prince Albert with muttonchop whiskers, a man whose god had been created in his own image, one who deemed failure an illness and illness a judgment from on high and who never in a long life had done a stroke of physical exercise. And there was Ezra Townsend, Myron's father, child of the founder's old age, conceived by that fashionable painter John Alexander as the suave adviser to the very rich in the day of the great Theodore, with brooding eyes and a drooping moustache, gray suede gloves held in one hand as if about to take polite leave of a valued but nonetheless tedious client, thin to the point of boniness, elegant, superior, bored. Was he already spending the capital of the family reputation? And answering the courteous but insistent queries of the younger partners with tales of his progenitor's old triumphs at the bar?

And finally there was Myron in a portrait by William Draper, which Myron, not the firm, had paid for. Gone now was any suggestion of law or law reports, of elegant oratory in the courtroom or less elegant bargaining in the conference chamber. Myron was seen as tall and finely built with thick, curled, prematurely gray hair at the wheel of his sailing yacht, his handsome profile facing into a marine breeze. And where were the clients? Left at the dock perhaps.

Well, at least there would be no more entries. The worst part of each business day in the last terrible two years had been quitting time. He had come actually to dread the moment when Mrs. Olyphant, his large, bland, elderly, remorselessly smiling secretary, or "executive assistant," as she preferred to style herself, would loom in his doorway, pad in hand, and announce, like a nurse shaking a bottle of despised medicine, "Time for entries, Mr. Townsend!"

When he had started to practice law, it had been the tolerated attitude of both partners and clerks to look down on the allotment of work to hours in the day, to regard the totaling of "chargeable time" as a wart on the fair countenance of a noble profession and to leave the vulgar business of billing to a largely invisible accounting staff supervised by a managing partner whose bizarre enthusiasm for such tedious matters was viewed with outward gratitude and inner contempt. But those were the days when clerks were paid less than stenographers. Now the computer, ruthless seeker-out of escalating overhead, was the powerful searchlight that beamed its deadly ray into every corner of the firm's activities to spy each dusty hour not lubricated with the winking gleam of gain.

"What *did* I do today, Mrs. Olyphant?"

"Well, there was Miss. Irwin's codicil."

"Ah, yes, of course. Put in three hours for that."

"I should have thought it was more like one. And you told the dear lady you wouldn't bill her more than a hundred bucks. If you charge her with that much time, you'll have to write most of it off, and accounting will want to know why."

"All right, all right. Put her down for one and charge two to Saint Joseph's Hospital."

"But there's that memo of Mr. Collins's, you know."

"What memo?"

"The one where he said he wanted to review all charitable clients whose hours topped a hundred in any one quarter. We've been putting an awful lot of hours on Saint Joseph's recently."

He knew she meant well. She loved working for a senior partner, and the social reputation of the Townsends appealed to her snobbish if amiable nature. But she knew perfectly how vulnerable he was. More belligerent than he, she believed he should assert his rank and refuse to send in any entries at all, and had so urged him, but so long as he dared not do this, she sought at least to minimize his misrepresentations.

"All right. Put in two hours for Office."

"Under what heading?"

"Just Office General."

She ventured a chuckle. "Isn't there a limit to how much more we can sweep under that carpet?"

He laughed in spite of himself. "You mean it's so lumpy now one can hardly walk on it? Very well. Put two hours under the heading of educating associates. I had to explain some things to Nat Danford."

But it was a mistake to have laughed with Mrs. Olyphant. She always took immediate and cheerful advantage of it. "Mr. Collins will be saying that young man should be paying tuition. We've put in more hours for him than a law school semester!"

Her use of "we" showed indeed how much she was on his side, but he suddenly could bear no more. "I'll do them tomorrow," he said testily as he rose.

"But you're behind three days now, sir!"

"Good night, Mrs. Olyphant!"

The end had come with a visit from Ralph Collins, a batch of computer print-outs draped ominously over his arm.

"I've been trying to get hold of you for a week now, Myron. You're a hard man to nail down."

"I've been pretty busy, Ralph."

"Have you now? Well, that's just what I want to talk to you about. A man can be awfully busy without making much money, and if that's the case, perhaps he should change something in his work habits. I've been going over your time sheets and comparing them with the income statements of your department."

Collins, pale, slight and balding, had shining, colorless eyes behind gold-rimmed spectacles. His eyes smiled too much. It was not, Myron surmised, really cruelty; it was hardly even amusement. It was rather the curiosity, quite removed from the irrelevance of either sympathy or dislike, of a scientist performing an interesting experiment. A senior partner who had survived his utility to the firm (if indeed he had ever had any), a representative of Knickerbocker New York, a Wasp, as the current term had it, was being presented with irrefutable evidence that the partnership bearing the name of his father and grandfather was losing more money than could be justified in maintaining his shrunken practice of trusts and estates. What would he say? How would he take it?

"I don't need to see the figures, Ralph," Myron snapped. "I assume they're quite dreadful. I shan't question them. I'll try to run a tighter ship. Next quarter should be better. The Sanford trust accounting should be ready for billing."

"The Sanford trust *has* been billed, Myron. It was billed last year, and the bank has questioned it. I am told we'll be lucky if we get paid half of it, and that will show the matter as a loss. But never mind the individual bills. The fact is, your department has been running in the red for three years now. Ever since the Bradley estate was closed. Do you see any more big estates like that coming in?"

"Well, I suppose there's always my wife's to look forward to," Myron observed, with heavy irony.

"Bella, I'm sure, will bury us all, and let us hope she does! But actually, Myron, didn't you once tell me that the bulk of her money is in trust? And that Milbank Tweed is counsel there?"

"It's true." Myron shrugged, ready now to give up the futile argument. "There'd be only peanuts for us to handle. What do you want, Ralph? To shut down the department? Isn't it an asset to a corporate law firm to have a general practice? How can we call ourselves lawyers if we can't even draw a will?"

"My dear Myron, we can always hire someone to do that. And, anyway, we live in an era of referrals. More and more firms are specializing. What I am finding it very difficult to justify to the younger partners at our weekly lunches (which, incidentally, you have been noticeably avoiding of late) is why you need two associates, two secretaries and an accountant to run a department that appears to be consistently losing money."

"Are there no such things as intangible values?"

"I note they tend to be cited by those who fail to produce tangible ones."

"And the fact that there's been a Townsend in the firm since 1875—that goes for nothing? How do you know, when a client walks past that door bearing my family's name to consult you about one of his mergers, that he isn't relying, at least in part, on the respectability that my father and grandfather gave the firm?"

"I don't know. But I do know that we live in a world that seems to care very little about the past. Everything is now, now, now. Take our balance sheets. The time was when we had to check them only at the end of the year. Then it was quarterly, then monthly, then weekly. And now I find myself asking our controller: Have we had a good *day*?"

"Isn't it all rather hysterical?"

"It is. But it's life. Even the biggest firms live so close to the line these days that with a couple of bad months they have to start thinking of laying people off."

"Well, certainly in estates we've already been cut to the bone. I couldn't run things with one less hand."

"I'm afraid you'll have to, Myron. We're eliminating a clerk, a secretary and the accountant."

"Good God!" Myron jumped to his feet. "You leave me with one lawyer and one girl! Who is going to do the work, I'd like to know?"

"I guess you are, Myron. And I'm afraid that's not all. We're cutting your percentage by a full half."

Myron gaped. "A third-year clerk will be making more than I will!"

"And bringing in more business, too, I'm afraid."

"Very well, Collins. I resign. As of today. And you can take my name off the letterhead. I don't care to have it associated with such a bunch of cheapskates."

Collins's smile was usually a fixed one, not really a smile at all, but now it broadened into a beam. "As to resigning, you must do as you see best. My terms stand if you change your mind. But we're not going to alter the firm name. That Townsend is not you, nor even perhaps your father. It's your grandfather. And I have little doubt that if he were here today, he'd be telling you what I've just told you."

That evening, over a cocktail, in their beautiful long white living room looking down on the East River, he told Arabella of his decision. She listened with her usual air of tranquillity, occasionally turning the thin gold bracelet on her left wrist. She rarely seemed surprised at anything he had to tell her; her small, neat, trim motionless figure, her smooth gray hair and the blue gaze of her calmly appraising eyes seemed ready for any contingency, at least that he might offer. She didn't look her sixty years because she didn't look any age. She was not so much pretty as perfect; her appearance suggested her philosophy of doing the best one could, the very best, with whatever material one had been given.

"Well, of course I think it's wonderful news. I've wanted you to retire for two years now.

"Two years? Why two?"

"Because you haven't had any pleasure in your work for the past two years. Perhaps even more, but I've noticed it only in that time."

Really, she was marvelous! When she seemed least to note she was most noting. In the five years of their marriage she had learned everything there was to know about him, and what had he learned about her that he hadn't already known?

"And what do we do now? Go round and round the world? On your money?"

"On *our* money, silly. But of course we won't do anything so ridiculous. What did Emerson say of travel? That it was taking ruins to ruins? I have a very different plan. One that I've had two years to think about."

Bella's fortune came from her mother, who had got it from hers. You had to go back to her great-grandfather to find the first earning male. This unusual situation, Myron had observed with a wry amusement, had created a curious attitude on her part about money. It was something that only women, trained women, really knew how to handle and spend. Men were apt to hoard it or blow it or dissipate it on things that didn't essentially make them happier.

He and she had lost their first mates to cancer; both had deemed themselves inconsolable. Friends had conspired to bring them together; the compatibility of similar tastes and difficult children (he had a radical daughter, she an alcoholic son) had tightened the initial bond of loneliness, and in their union they had found a life of peacefulness and early hours.

"I've been thinking of the plea you got to head up the fund drive for the Staten Island Zoo," she told him. "Why not take that on? You love that zoo, and now you're going to have the time to do it. I have an idea that you might make a great fund raiser. You've always worried about your ability to make money for yourself. Why not show people that you can make it for others?"

"Bella!" he exclaimed in astonishment. "What an interesting

idea! Have you been nursing it for long?"

"I've been waiting till you were ready. And now let's get on with it. I think you're going to need your old office. I'll rent it from Ralph Collins. Don't worry. I'll know how to handle him. And Mrs. Olyphant. She'll be a great hand at this game."

Myron began to feel that a whole wonderful new life was being placed squarely, perhaps even a bit heavily, in his taken-for-granted lap. But mightn't this be what happiness was?

"Bella," he asked in sudden suspicion, "have you been discussing this project with Mrs. Olyphant?"

She simply smiled and suggested that they celebrate the occasion with a rare second cocktail.

And so his new life started.

The beginning was simple enough. His offer to take the chairmanship of the major fund drive about to be launched by the Staten Island Zoological Gardens, of whose board he had long been a devoted member, was, needless to say, gratefully accepted, and Ralph Collins, deftly handled by the tactful Bella, was found agreeable to the idea of having a Townsend back in his office at no cost to the firm, indeed, actually paying rent. If Collins was still not wholly convinced of the "intangible values" of an old name, he was perfectly willing to pick up any such values that came free. Mrs. Olyphant, moreover, proved superb and efficient in her new role. Free of the nagging interference of an office manager, she roundly snubbed the secretaries of the younger partners, who had once tossed in her face that their bosses paid for hers. And at the zoo offices, to which she repaired on alternate afternoons, she trained the girls in public relations in how to address rich potential donors—and in how to pronounce their names. Her years of reading the social columns in magazines and evening journals became a distinct asset to the drive.

Myron found that he loved the work. His rich friends and relatives, who had regarded him, a bit ruefully, as too much the easygoing club gentleman to be entrusted with the thorny tax planning of their estates, were delighted to find that they could oblige him by contributing to an institution in which many of them were anyway interested. And Myron did much more than just solicit them. He would take them, one by one, to an excellent lunch in a private dining room in the zoo's administration building, followed by a visit "behind the scenes" to see a baby elephant born or the big cats hosed or a polar bear operated on or whatever the particular event of the day happened to be.

In time he learned to match the exhibition to the particular taste of the visitor. The ladies liked the little furry animals, the more brightly colored birds and the young of almost any species. The men preferred the large dangerous predators. Sometimes Myron, suspecting a sadistic streak, would take a corporation president to see mice eaten by snakes, and for the lewdly inclined the monkeys could always be counted on to copulate. The keepers had been told to produce, if feasible, what Myron asked for, and the only time he had a serious row with the director was when a proposed "spat" between two leopards had got out of control and resulted in the serious mauling of one of the beasts.

The money poured in. Myron was quick to pick up the tricks of his new trade: to get the poorer trustees to pledge more than they could pay (with private assurance they would not be dunned) so that the richer ones would not feel they were being stuck with the whole load; to name the first baby of any species to be born in captivity after a generous lady (with much publicity); to whisper in the ear of one tycoon that another, his particular rival, was pledging twice his sum; to abrogate the names of buildings and wings as soon as the donor's family had become extinct or obscure, so as to have more tags available for new givers; to sell positions on the organizing committees of benefit parties to social climbers and even a seat at Amy Bledsoe's table for twenty-five g's.

Bella herself now took on the job of chairman of a big drive for the Manhattan Gallery of Art, of which she had long been a trustee, and centered her activities in Townsend, Cox & Collins, where she rented an office next to her husband's. "We'll be known as Mr. and Mrs. New York," she said with mock smugness. Ralph Collins's tongue seemed to drip as he noted the passage through the reception hall of some of the biggest names in town. Surely some of these might stick! Myron found himself now invited to the firm lunches he had not dared to attend when he was a nonproducing partner.

It was intoxicating. He had always been deeply mortified by his inability to make big money in a money society, and even when he had, on rare occasions, got his hands on a large fee, he had been haunted by the sense that he had not really earned it, that it had been simply based on a percentage of an estate that had come to the firm through an earlier Townsend. But now he discovered—or Bella discovered for him (he was happy to give her full credit)—an ability in himself, which nobody could challenge, of raising sums far larger than any partner of his old firm could have dreamed of charging as a fee. He was their equal at last, and it wasn't just because he was Sidney Townsend's grandson, either. Staring boldly at the latter's portrait as he strode through the reception hall, he asked himself with a complaisant sneer who in the world would have given so mean-looking an old codger a blasted nickel no matter what worthy cause he was touting!

Myron and Bella carried their work into the evening hours. She had always been less critical than he of dull parties so long as they were, as she put it, "well done." Ever a keen observer of food, wine, service and décor, the latter including the gowns of her hostess and the lady guests, she was inclined to forgive bad talk for good appearance. And of course, as a museum trustee, she could put up with the fiercest bore if his walls were hung with masterpieces and his table covered with fine porcelain. But now she shared with Myron a single criterion: their hosts had to be wealthy or have wealthy guests. Dinner parties were no longer dull play; they had become stimulating work. Even if they took up every evening in the week, they never palled.

The only difficulty was in not appearing too available to the socially ambitious and thus watering their stock-in-trade.

"I heard you telling Silas Hofritz that we'd be glad to come to his seventieth birthday party," Bella noted in the car as they were returning from a dinner where they had met that particularly odoriferous developer. "When the invitation comes in, I suggest you tell Mrs. Olyphant to call his secretary and say you'd forgotten we were going to the country that day. That will show him we

SHORT STORY INTERNATIONAL

prefer a simple rural excursion to his great gala."

Myron meekly accepted the reproach. "I thought as soon as I'd said it that I might have been going too far."

"A man like that would at once assume that we weren't the real Townsends. That we'd probably changed our name. He thinks his money can buy him anything, and it can, in time, but he's got to put it up first, and plenty of it. That's our job."

"I'll be more careful in future. What is lowlier than an unpaid prostitute?"

Bella ignored his question. She didn't like him to be *quite* so cynical. "We may go to Mr. Hofritz's *next* birthday. Or drop in for a drink and not stay for dinner. In the meanwhile why don't you take him to a zoo lunch? Do the crocodiles ever eat each other? That might be his affair."

"Yet he goes to Amy's."

"That's different. Amy's like royalty. She can afford to have *anybody.*"

Amy Bledsoe, who had become an intimate friend of the Townsends, occupied a unique position in Gotham. She had no claim to it in looks or birth. She was an elderly stout woman of middle-class Irish origin who dyed her abundant billowing hair a flaming red and wore large jewels that went oddly with her plain sensible countenance. She had been first the trained nurse, then the housekeeper and at last the wife and widow of Horace Bledsoe, the investment banker, who had left her the "big" half of his estate in a marital deduction trust, the balance going to his son and daughter by an earlier marriage. It was the opinion of those who knew her best that Amy had never been the old man's mistress. She was shrewd, well read, big-hearted and full of sound common sense, and she gave widely and intelligently from her large income. But the peculiar veneration with which she was regarded by the New York social world sprang less from her generosity, which, after all, could easily be topped by multimillionaire friends who could give from principal as well as income, as from her robust character, from her virtuousness (to use a word they never would), from something anyway that made her a kind of saint in a desert that might have been tired of too many lizards and scorpions.

Amy gave generously to both Myron's zoo and Bella's gallery, but when she complained one evening, when he was seated on her right at one of her dinner parties, that her ability to support charities would cease with her death, an idea struck him, and he became for a moment quite tense with concentration.

"You mean because what you have is in trust?"

"Yes. It's what they call a marital deduction trust. It all has to go to Horace's children when I die."

"Who already have millions."

"And who are not renowned, I fear, for their philanthropy."

"But don't you have the power to appoint the trust principal?"

"But that's just a technicality. The law made Horace give me that if the trust was not to be taxed in his estate. I promised him I'd never exercise it, and of course I never will."

"Hmm." Myron's heart was pounding. He even found a moment to reflect that his new idea had made him the superior of his father and grandfather. "Tell me, Amy. Hasn't the principal of your trust gone up in value since Horace's death?"

"Oh, it's more than doubled!"

"Then I suggest that your promise is limited to the date of death value. I can see no reason that you shouldn't feel free to appoint the increase as you see fit. And I'll bet Horace would have agreed."

Amy's mouth fell open as she stared at him. "Why, Myron Townsend, what a brilliant idea! I see what you mean. It's as if I'd somehow earned that increase. Except of course I didn't. The trustees are two of Horace's most brilliant partners."

"That makes no difference. They were working for you. You can simply add a paragraph to your will that you appoint any percentage of the trust principal that exceeds the value of the trust at your husband's death to..."

"The Staten Island Zoological Gardens!" Amy exclaimed, clapping her hands.

Something cautioned him to restrain her. "Or in equal shares to the zoo and Bella's gallery," he added with a laugh, as if to make a jest of it.

"Of course, the children will howl."

"But you won't be there to hear them."

"No, I'll be in the special heaven reserved for the ultraphilanthropic!"

Was she laughing at him? It was hard to tell with Amy. But if she was serious, O gun at sea, O bells that in the steeples be, at first repeat it slow! Myron loved Emily Dickinson. He would raise a hundred million for his and Bella's institutions! He almost regretted now having to divide with Bella. But if Amy were to consult with Bella about the plan, it would be as well to place a carrot under his wife's more scrupulous nose.

And Amy was indeed going to discuss the matter with Bella. That was what she was now telling him, before she had to turn to the man on her left.

"I want you and Bella to stay on for a bit tonight after the others have left."

Myron sat after dinner with Bella in an agony of apprehension, the last guest having left, waiting for their hostess, who had briefly excused herself.

"I think I've figured out the greatest common denominator of Amy's group," Bella observed pensively.

"Ambition perhaps? Satisfied ambition?"

"Is ambition ever satisfied? No, I think what makes them different is that they all speak so glowingly of one another."

"Only when they're here, though. The moment they're out of Amy's sight, they tear each other to bits."

"So Amy's is a place of suspended hostilities. That dreadful little new wife of Sam Spatz hadn't the faintest idea who I was tonight, but she bent over backwards to be polite. If you're at Amy's, I guess, you can't be nobody."

"Isn't it possible that they simply want to convince themselves that they really are what they only seem at Amy's? Even the cultural crowd who are on the prowl for grants. Amy cleans them up! For a whole euphoric evening, they can almost forget the wear and tear of acquisition. Going to Amy's for them is like going to church."

"And what is it like for you and Bella?" Amy was standing in the doorway with a scolding smile.

"We don't have to go to church," Myron responded as he rose to greet her. "We're already there. Acolytes at your altar."

She crossed the floor slowly and slumped in the sofa by Bella, contemplating the empty chamber with a sigh of relief. "Thanks for staying on." And she proceeded now to tell the expressionless but attentively listening Bella the details of Myron's proposal.

Bella's face still reflected nothing when Amy finished and sat regarding her inquisitively.

"Will you discuss this with Horace's children?"

"No, because I know what they'd say. They'd say I had no moral right to do it. But I shouldn't care what they thought if I was sure in my own mind that what I was doing was right. What would you do, Bella, if you found yourself in my situation?"

"If you put it that way, I have to tell you I wouldn't exercise the power." Bella's tone was light, perhaps a bit self-consciously light. "Not even to deflect a penny from those already overendowed darlings. You're perfectly clear that you wouldn't reduce the principal going to them below its value at Horace's death, aren't you?"

"Oh, of course, that's sacred!"

"And why? Because that was Horace's clearly expressed intent. But didn't he expect that principal to increase in value? Didn't he spend his whole business life making money multiply itself? Didn't he make his smartest partners your trustees? If he had meant you to give any of that anticipated growth to charities, wouldn't he have told you so?"

"Oh, Bella, you're wonderful!" Amy clapped her hands in evident relief. "Of course, you're right as right can be. I have been so worried that maybe it was my duty to give some of that money to good causes. My duty to Horace himself! And now of course I see it would be a shocking breach of faith. Oh, my dear, I shall sleep so much better tonight. The whole horrid business has been taken right out of my hands."

Myron was too shocked by the sudden slamming of shutters on so briefly glimpsed a horizon of shimmering beauty to say anything for a minute. He would need time to reflect on the matter. It was better now to make light of it.

"I guess this shows I've spent too much time with my animals. In the jungle one is less burdened with scruples. Everything eats everything!"

"And darling Bella, with her love of beautiful inanimate things, has the more delicate moral sense! Oh, how I see it! But I've kept you poor dears up long enough. You must go home now, and God bless you both!"

Their chauffeur was not separated from them by a glass, so it was natural enough that they should not speak of personal matters, but even so Myron felt sure that Bella was very conscious of the fact that they were not doing so. Even in their apartment they refrained. He simply offered her a cordial good night kiss before retreating to his own room. But then, on an impulse, he turned back.

"Bella. Are you perfectly sure that you gave Amy the right advice tonight?"

Ah, she had been waiting for that! Her eyes were fixed on his. "Perfectly."

"You don't think it's better that all those millions should go to our beloved zoo and gallery than to two arrogant and selfish people, already millionaires several times over?"

"Better? Of course, it would be better. But is that our decision? Amy gave her solemn pledge to her husband. I wouldn't urge her to break it to save our institutions from utter ruin!"

"Bella! How can you be that extreme?"

"Because, unlike you, I don't believe that ends, however shining, justify means, however filthy. Because I've seen your eyes grow hard as agates in the last two years. It's my fault, of course. I got you started in this game. But that's just why it's my job to pull you out."

He gazed at her in dismay. "Amy was right. You're as pure as a Ming vase."

"And as hard. Go on. Say it."

"And as hard."

"Perhaps something was left out of my nature. I've always preferred beautiful things to ordinary people. But not, I hope, to beautiful people. And, oh, my dear!" She was actually appealing to him now! "I have thought of you as a beautiful person. I can't bear to have you become an ugly one. Promise me that you won't become an ugly one!"

He stared. "What do you mean?"

"Don't go back to Amy and work on her to change her mind!"

"You think I was planning to?"

"Weren't you?"

The heaviness of his sigh showed that he had given it up. "All right. I won't." He paused. "I'll promise you that I won't. And like Amy I won't break it. Even, as you say, if our institutions should go to hell."

And going now to his room, he decided that he had, after all, married a remarkable woman.

The gifted Louis Stanton Auchincloss' intelligence and charm are reflected in his work. He is a highly respected attorney in New York City, President of the Museum of the City of New York, a member of the National Institute of Arts and Letters and the author of 40 works of fiction and non-fiction. His story "The Senior Partner's Ethics" appeared in SSI No. 75.

"Finally, he confessed to Ruth what had happened without telling her the most horrific detail..."

Life Game

BY UYEN LOEWALD

DAVID Cohen stands in front of the Life Game Restaurant, stunned. He can barely remember his mission: to attend the international conference on chemical warfare. Everything looks unchanged. Everything reminds him of the past. Saigon is as teasing now as it was then. The only visible differences are the absence of American GIs and European and American cars, which have been replaced by motorcycles. Of course, he must admit that the women don't look as beautiful now as they did then, but they still look charming, even disarming.

He feels the blood rushing to his cheeks as he quickly enters the air-conditioned room, and signals to the Vietnamese waitress wearing a dai, which displays two lines of brown silky skin on either side. It's twenty years later and having seen, touched, felt, cut and stitched up so many different kinds of skin, he is still unable to forget the sensation he felt when his body touched the smooth coolness of Vietnamese femininity. He tries not to think of

Saigon so personally. But medicine is a personal subject. Its personal aspect determines the physician's degree of professional competence, commitment and dedication.

Was it mere dedication that time? The 1968 Tet Offensive left deep emotional scars on doctors: a group of German physicians were executed by the Vietcong because the leader was suspected of spying for the CIA. It was never proven one way or another. But the man's son was a CIA agent. Hearing the fate of those German doctors on arrival had pushed David Cohen and his team off balance. He can still feel the emptiness, the shame, the sense of failure, the fear of losing self-control again.

He had kept wondering whether other doctors felt that way. But he was too shy to ask. A Jew living in the city of pork and shellfish where Jews were mistaken for wanderers, he was totally unconnected.

It took him awhile to train his cook not to use lard in preparing his kosher meals. After exhausting efforts, he gave up the idea of training Vietnamese servants to keep a kosher kitchen. One concession led to another. When David Cohen had arrived in Saigon, his body longed for conjugal intimacy. He did not expect that having seen prepared, anesthetized, and partially exposed flesh every day, he would be preoccupied with fantasy about Vietnamese slimness under graceful traditional costumes.

He remembers the event as clearly as if it were just happening. He can still feel that exciting indignation when one of his colleagues, the man he came to replace, said: "The brothel just offered me the most beautiful sixteen year old virgin from Quang Nam. Her mother sold her for 500 piasters, but they want $500 from me to make 199% profit. Since I am leaving for Los Angeles next week, that price becomes exorbitant. You should take her. Of course, you must examine her first. Virgins are a little bit more expensive, but they're STD proof." The man rattled on. "If she is as exciting as the madam said, she'll make a sensational hostess."

The war stimulated diplomatic imagination: every spouseless diplomat in Saigon procured a hostess who would live with him and entertain his guests as the lady of the house. Consequently, as American men found Vietnamese women irresistible, loneliness compounded with infrequent matrimonial visits and reluctant sexual dissatisfaction pushed many American wives off the edge. One was given a lobotomy and became a vegetable; two became alcoholic, then were put in an institution for schizophrenics; another repeatedly attempted suicide until she successfully killed herself. Like the heroin trade, diplomatic casualties went on long after the Vietnam War ended.

Nothing like that would ever happen to him, David Cohen had promised himself. He felt so ashamed of humanity, of his profession. He was still proud of statistical records of his culture then: more Jewish women entered marriage as virgins than women of any other faith. From his limited knowledge of Vietnam, virginity was not only highly regarded but also essential for a woman's marriage prospects and reputation. Doctors were healers, not killers, he kept reminding his colleagues and himself.

He had started his mission in Vietnam with a debate on brothels and madams and virgin prostitutes and medical responsibilities. As the debate went on aimlessly, compared to the indiscriminate killing by war of thousands of men, women and children, Vietnamese culture and virginity became more and more insignificant. Medically speaking, it would only hinder women's pleasure. At best it was men's misplaced pride.

David Cohen would have nothing to do with prostitutes, especially virgin prostitutes. The thought of entering a brothel repelled him.

But war and survival required immediate and practical actions. He decided to buy the prostitute and send her to school while he would train her as a community worker to help other unfortunate girls like herself. David Cohen felt so proud, so practical. In the past he had depended on his mother, then his wife, to make minor decisions. Now he gave $500 to Neil White to rescue the innocent girl from the most ancient barbarism.

The more David Cohen tries to forget the more clearly he remembers the day Mme. Liane brought Cam to his villa. It took him some time to collect himself for he had instantly lost his surgical calmness. He wanted the woman to convey his good intentions to Cam, but he failed to detain her. She snatched the

$500 and disappeared.

He showed the girl the spare bedroom. Realizing that she had no luggage, he pointed to the living room, telling her in English and gestures that she should wait for him there while he went to the shops to buy some of the things she would need.

By the time he returned with some change of clothes, a tooth brush and tooth paste, Cam had miraculously transformed his ostentatious but impersonal living room into a tasteful home, something that could have been advertised in the *New Yorker*. A mixture of exotic and primitive art.

Cam said something to him in a sing-song way as she bowed and took the packet. When she saw the sky blue nightgown, she blushed. Clumsily she took his hand and pulled him towards the spare bedroom. He could not remember whether he was briefed or had read that Vietnamese tradition forbade men to touch women. He shrugged it off; there was no language between them; she must have wanted to show him another pleasant surprise. He used his free hand to tell her how she had made a home for him, touching his heart. Cam looked away from him as she touched his chest, stroking his thick hair and giggled, the same giggle as his wife's on their first date. He could only imagine Cam's thoughts.

By the time he understood what Cam intended to do, it was too late. He could no longer control his desire. David Cohen was awakened by the pungent fishy smell from the kitchen. As his feet reached the tile floor, he noticed a spread of blood on the white sheet. Shame became tears; he pulled the sheet off. Cam rushed in from the kitchen, took the sheet from his hands and soaked it in the bathtub. Obediently he let her pull him by the hand to the dining room. She served him beef soup with lemon grass.

"Are you pleased?"

Cam's first sentence in English surprised him. She giggled again with the same melody which, overnight, became part of his existence. It removed his loneliness. He began to fear that she might leave him. Every cell in his body had undergone a radical change.

When Cam went out to buy ingredients to prepare breakfast, she also bought a book for herself to learn English. Some weeks later, Cam became sick one morning. In broken English she asked him to give her something to calm her stomach. He examined her then gave her a blood test only to discover, to his horror, that she was pregnant. What an irony: the first and only unprotected extramarital sex with an innocent teen-ager had left an experienced doctor in tatters.

There was no time to waste; instead of discussing a plan for her education, he suggested an abortion.

Cam listened to the interpreter. Tears flooded her eyes; her healthy color left her face; her entire body shook as she spoke. Waiting for the interpreter's words was interminable. "Please, I know that you have bought me and paid such a large sum of money for me and that I have promised Mme. Liane that I will stay here with you until you leave for the U.S. But I never expected that I would be in this situation. I beg you to allow me to keep the baby. If you don't want the baby, I would rather kill myself so that my baby and I will die together and our souls will remain unseparated." She went on as he succumbed to emotion.

He could ask her neither to leave nor to have an abortion. Through the Army interpreter, she promised that she would never make any demands on him and would never come between him and his family. "I have no right to ask for anything. My parents sold me to the brothel; you have saved my life. I had no honor, so I have no shame. No one knows me."

He interrupted her with kisses. Suddenly he became acutely aware that he was observing himself the way psychologists observe laboratory mice. He had never been able to imagine that anyone could express love to another person through an interpreter. He began to understand the meaning of war, of what the feminists had accused men of doing. War meant rape. He had raped this innocent country girl who looked, he could only imagine, as Mona Lisa would have looked. But she had not resisted. She had not even uttered a sound. Would she have protested if there had been an interpreter? Was she conditioned to being raped? His country was raping her country; what he had been doing was only to epitomize what his country, the most powerful country in the world, was doing. With amazing detachment he had undressed his soul to a stranger.

As if the interpreter understood his mind, he said, "Dr. Cohen, you are not the first and you will not be the last to have had sexual intercourse with a Vietnamese minor, but don't worry. My stupid country is so corrupt that it couldn't care less. As a matter of fact, if you like, you can even charge her with spying for the Communists." The interpreter laughed like a drunkard.

The telephone roared: "Dr Cohen, a Marine needs immediate surgery."

There was no time for moral issues, war or peace. He had to reassure the wounded soldier, decide on the length of the incision, the optimum pressure to control bleeding while keeping his tissues alive. He was trained to dissect, stitch, and treat different segments of the human body as separate parts of a mysterious whole, to save those which were worth saving, to discard those which were beyond hope, and to recycle them for experiment in the hope to advance science or obtain the Nobel Prize.

Like his country, David Cohen went to Vietnam to do good, to save lives, to defend democracy and to reduce suffering. Now he is on his way to the surgery—leaving Cam behind, abused, lonely, desperate and bewildered.

Another life was saved but David Cohen did not feel like celebrating. All he could only think of was Cam, hoping that the interpreter was still with her, and that he had been asked to wait. The chauffeur honked as the car weaved among motorcycles, taxis and cyclos during the hours when most people should still be in bed.

The interpreter and Cam greeted David Cohen with calm smiles. "Cam wants me to tell you that she would be honored to be your mistress; she promises to ask for nothing, except a safe place for her and the baby until you leave Vietnam. The baby is yours, and Vietnamese custom dictates that the woman follows her husband. You are her husband in Vietnamese tradition, but since you married her without your official wife's consent, she cannot expect to be allowed to live with you. She leaves you to decide whether you will take your child along if it is a boy."

Again David Cohen lost his composure. The thought of his mother's reaction if he told her he was going to return with a half-Vietnamese son chilled him, although secretly he hoped for a son. He had approached his wife on this matter a few times but she was adamant on two children. "What's wrong with our two beautiful daughters?" Ruth had brushed the subject aside. He could understand; she had finally established herself as a pediatrician. David Cohen missed his children unbearably. Would they understand that their father lost control over an under-aged girl? He must write to Ruth as he promised he would write to her every day. He had been in Saigon less than two months. He had written her at least a dozen letters. But words had not come to him easily. She would understand. It would take her that long to decide what carpet to buy.

Everything became so absurd. Until he was asked to go to Vietnam, although he did glance at the *New York Times* once in awhile, he never paid much attention to it. It was a terrible war, he agreed with Ruth. "The sooner we pull out the better." But shopping, choosing interior decor, replacing the carpet not because it was worn but because it needed to be replaced so that the colors in the house would be better coordinated, preoccupied their conversation. At first their congregation carefully avoided the Vietnam War because Israel needed American aid, then he was too busy with his practice to notice. One matter followed another.

David Cohen wished he were not a perfectionist and a patriot: he combined the opportunity to gain professional experience with his contribution to humanity. Whether he was convicted or not, whether it became known or not, he was guilty of rape. Yet he did not feel disgusted with himself as he should feel or he had imagined what a man ought to feel in case of rape.

Through the interpreter, he told Cam that they should decide together: "We have seven more months to sort out our situation. I am sorry to put her in such a mess." David Cohen was surprised by his own words. "I would like Cam to go to school to learn English and whatever she wants to learn. I'll pay for everything. I will also give her $100 a month for pocket money. When the baby comes, I will give her more money. Everything for the baby will be provided. Please ask her whether she has any questions."

The interpreter told David Cohen that Cam thanked him: "She promises you that she will not disappoint you. She will learn English quickly so that she can communicate with you directly. She wants to please you. She wants to know whether you would like her to become a Christian because white men are Christians. She is a Buddhist, but Vietnamese custom says she must accept her husband's religion. She is happy to do that."

David Cohen could not suppress his laugh: "She should learn Hebrew and keep a kosher house." He waved his hand: "Forget that."

But it was too late, Cam wanted to know what kosher meant and how she could learn Hebrew. She wanted to keep a kosher house for him, to raise his son according to his religion and culture.

Cam learned everything as fast as her stomach grew. Her morning sickness lasted only two weeks. Unlike his wife, Cam enjoyed being pregnant and did not gain weight despite her enormous appetite. She must have eaten her equivalent in weight every week. She became taller and more Western every day. Six months later, she was fluent in English. Her grammatical error and incorrect pronunciation here and there only made her even more irresistible. In no time, Cam became not only the most popular but also the most well-informed hostess. She possessed the ability to absorb and disseminate knowledge like a computer.

Cam gave birth to identical twins, who looked like David. She was remarkably correct; she would remind him every morning to write to Ruth, saying how much he loved her and longed for the day they would reunite. At first, the exercise was painful; he would sit for hours, listening to the twins cooing or crying for attention, but Cam would not allow him to neglect his matrimonial obligation: "I am lucky, I have two sons. Your wife is unlucky, she has two daughters. You must think of her. I am a woman, I know how she must feel. You must search your heart for the love and affection you had for her before you met me. I wish I spoke English then; we would have avoided all this heartache for you." She would kiss him.

Eventually, Cam became bolder; she would tell him what to write, thinking she might be Ruth waiting for her husband in New York, addressing all the fears and concerns Ruth might have. His relationship with Ruth couldn't have been better. Each letter from Ruth was more loving and understanding than the last. He fell in love with his wife again and again as if she were the mistress. He fell in love with the world despite the war. David Cohen went home every major holiday to be with his wife and children. When he returned to Vietnam, he would bring along all the presents his wife and daughters bought for the poor Vietnamese women and children, innocent victims of the war.

Living in two different worlds was as simple and as delicious as a dream. Ruth never questioned him because she understood that he had not written regularly during the early months because he needed time to settle down to a routine, and Cam continued to make his life in Vietnam worth living.

When David asked Ruth to let him extend his tour, she agreed without hesitation. He was the exemplary husband. Most husbands would write to their wives regularly at first, then, when they started to have mistresses on the side, their letters would become more infrequent, but David was the opposite. The distance had improved their communication. His frequent trips home and his passion for her increased with each trip to prove his commitment not only to her and the children but also to their faith.

The Paris talks gained some success. Kissinger received a Nobel Prize for Peace. David was relieved that Cam decided to remain in Vietnam. They spent the last days together in tears. Cam was firm. She had no right to ask for more. She had already spent three happy years in luxury. She no longer had to fear hunger. She was confident that, although her life would be lonely and perhaps even unhappy, she would be able to survive and she felt proud that she did not cause misery to another woman. She wanted to earn meritorious deeds so that her sons would be blessed.

David left Saigon with a heavy heart but, like Cam, he was confident that she and the twins would be safe as peace was just a matter of time. Saigon was no longer in danger. He made Cam promise that she would contact him through his best friend if she or the children needed help.

At first returning to New York was not as difficult as David had anticipated. His parents, sister and friends planned one celebration after another, as if he had just returned from the dead. They kept reminding him that he was with them to stay. Even those words did not sink in until the holiday and celebrations were over, when he started to hear the twins' crying voice and Cam's incomprehensible labor pain. He would wake up in the middle of the night in a cold sweat. The next morning he would write to people in Saigon and ask them to look for Cam, to report to him how his sons were doing. The most difficult time was the morning after the nightmare. His wife would try to comfort him: "I know how hard it must have been; you're such a conscientious doctor. You must have lost a few lives because of makeshift conditions..." The more his wife tried to comfort him, the worse he felt. David became totally absorbed in his work. His psychiatric friends also tried to help him. They could understand; thousands of combat soldiers returned from Vietnam with serious personality changes. Although David was a surgeon trained to cope with casualty, what doctor could cope with seeing how lives were wasted every day? But David refused all medication. He was even more horrified when one of his colleagues suggested hypnotherapy as the nightmares became more and more unbearable. David rejected their offer at first, fearing the truth might come out. But his nights became sheer torture: he would go to bed exhausted, drop off to sleep immediately while thinking how he could perform his matrimonial duty. He loved Ruth, but love, emotion and sensuality seemed to become disconnected.

His friend from Saigon wrote to him that he could not trace Cam. She had moved to the country and left no address. "The memory would be too much for her. She is probably married to someone now. She is so beautiful. What can you expect? She is not even twenty yet." There were more stories about other Americans, even a young army doctor who offered to marry her, but she turned every offer down.

Nightmares would wake him up. His eyes would feel sandy. He

was unable to function professionally. David Cohen consented to the experimental treatment: blocking out his painful memory of Vietnam and the war.

Life became more or less normal again. Although the relationship with his wife could never be the same as that during his tour in Vietnam or at the beginning of his return home, there was no reason for his wife to suspect that another woman was involved. He spent all his time between home and his practice; he attended to his children's needs.

The medical circle concluded that he suffered from a rare psychological disorder. Time and time again they asked for his permission to publish an article about it in the *Medical Journal*, but to protect his privacy, he refused.

Finally, David's wife accepted his mother's advice: "Try to give him a son. You know how important sons are. Surprise him. After all, you're a doctor. You know how to do it. I'll make sure that you lose no time in your practice. I'll personally take good care of my grandson."

The news that his wife was pregnant made him feel as guilty as the discovery that Cam was a minor. Poor Ruth, she wanted to save their marriage. All tests proved that the pregnancy was safe even though Ruth had reached the critical age. The children were excited about their little baby brother or sister. Shopping trips for baby things alternated with presents from every state. Massaging Ruth's stomach reminded David of Cam's wrinkle-free body. He became excited again. He made love to Ruth while thinking of Cam. It was a bitter-sweet experience.

Ruth gave birth to a son just after the fall of Saigon. Instead of celebrating his fortune, with immense effort, David could barely retain his sanity. Having a son while two others could have been killed! He cursed himself for being so stupid, for not having gone to Saigon to rescue his family.

Finally, he confessed to Ruth what had happened without telling her the most horrific detail: Cam was under age!

Ruth agreed to a divorce. David surrendered his property to Ruth to make up for all the pain he caused her. He was unable to relate to his son. He started his life from scratch; he joined the

Physicians for Social Justice and Peace Now, and has been doing research on peace and rehabilitation.

David is stunned by all the artifacts displayed in the Life Game Restaurant. They are unmistakably those he had given to Cam when they lived together. Could she be the owner of the restaurant? It's too much to hope for. But how can the collection be so complete? She probably sold it before marrying or moving out of town. He must ask the owner.

David sits down at the table near the most beautiful painting of Cam when she was two months pregnant, his Mona Lisa. Resting his head against the wall he can identify the melody of Cam's voice. It must come from some room upstairs, distant but clear, like a recorded message. It's a little more mature, but the same. Unmistakably hers. She is talking on the phone in English. Her husband? No, the words as well as the tone are affectionate but void of sexual implication. Someone living in another country. Someone close to her but not a lover or a husband. Cam laughs, the giggle kind of laughter which attracted him to her and which recurs in his dreams. "See you soon. All the best with your exams."

David stands up as he sees Cam walk down the circular stairs. As she sees him she stops, one hand still in mid-air, the other on the rail. David runs to her, holds her and covers her with kisses before he realizes she might not be free. She does not react, just as she did not react when he raped her. David still shivers when he thinks of the word.

At last, in a calm voice. she speaks: "I was wondering whether I should see you when I go to New York. The government allows people to go overseas as tourists provided someone overseas pays for the trip."

"Please do, I'll pay for the trip, any trip."

"No," she laughs. "It will not be necessary. Harvard has done that." She hesitates: "Our sons can also do it. Actually, it will be a feasibility study trip." She speaks to him in Hebrew, telling him how she knows all about his Jewish religion. But she asks him to tell her about his family first.

When David finishes his life story, Cam tells him she had changed her name to start a new life. Realizing that she had reached the age when middle-class women entered tertiary education, she went to Can Tho and employed a qualified teacher to help her pass the second *bachot* as she had passed the first shortly after his departure. She studied sociology at the University in Can Tho, with a specialty in prostitution because she had been sold as a prostitute. She wanted to do what he had planned for her.

She had joined the Communists. When the war in Vietnam ended, she organized the re-education of women addicts. "When the American Government allowed women who had children by Americans to go to the U.S., I decided to let our sons go. They deserve better opportunities. But I remain because I will not benefit from the government which deprived my people of the right to a decent living, and I must not disrupt your life. I told the embassy that their father is unknown because I was a prostitute. I used most of the money you gave me to buy this restaurant and employ some of the women I have rehabilitated." Cam smiles. She looks older, but age agrees with her. "Would you like to see the children's photographs."

"Yes, please." David tries to contain tears as Cam leads him upstairs by the hand. No clumsiness, no hesitation. "They look just like you; they want to study medicine. They will be so happy when I tell them I found you."

Born in 1940, in Haiduong (near Hanoi), Uyen Loewald went to South Vietnam in 1951. She was a student of literature and mathematics in Saigon. In 1962 she was imprisoned by the Diem Regime. She is currently in Australia. Her story "Patriotism" appeared in SSI No. 89.

For readers who can't read...

Greek, Arabic, Chinese, Japanese, Dutch, Norwegian, Chukchi, Finnish, Hindi, Turkish, Urdu, Hebrew, Russian, Vietnamese, Portuguese, etc., etc.

Short Story International takes you to all points of the compass, to anywhere in the world. There are intriguing stories waiting for you in future issues of SSI—stories that will involve you in corners of this world you've never seen...and in worlds outside this one...with glimpses into the future as well as the past, revealing fascinating, universal truths that bypass differences in language and point up similarities in people.

Send in the coupon below and every other month SSI will take you on a world cruise via the best short stories being published throughout the world today—the best entertainment gleaned from the work of the great creative writers who are enhancing the oldest expression of the entertainment arts—the short story.

A Harvest of the World's
Best Contemporary Writing Selected
and Published Every Other Month

Please enter my subscription to
Short Story International
P.O. Box 405, Great Neck, New York 11022
Six Issues for $24, U.S. & U.S. Possessions
Canada $27 (US), All Other Countries $29 (US)
Enclosed is my check for $ _____ for _____ subscriptions.

Name _____

Address _____

City _____ State _____ Zip _____

Country _____

Please check ☐ *New Subscription* ☐ *Renewal*

Gift for:
Name _____
Address _____
City _____State_____ Zip_____
Country _____ _____
Please check ☐ New Subscription   ☐ Renewal

Gift for:
Name _____
Address _____
City _____State_____ Zip_____
Country _____
Please check ☐ New Subscription   ☐ Renewal

Gift for:
Name _____
Address _____
City _____State_____ Zip_____
Country _____
Please check ☐ New Subscription   ☐ Renewal

Gift for:
Name _____
Address _____
City _____State_____ Zip_____
Country _____
Please check ☐ New Subscription   ☐ Renewal

Gift for:
Name _____
Address _____
City _____State_____ Zip_____
Country _____
Please check ☐ New Subscription   ☐ Renewal

Gift for:
Name _____
Address _____
City _____State_____ Zip_____
Country _____
Please check ☐ New Subscription   ☐ Renewal

For the young people in your life...

The world of the short story for young people is inviting, exciting, rich in culture and tradition of near and far corners of the earth. You hold the key to this world...a world you can unlock for the young in your life...and inspire in them a genuine love for reading. We can think of few things which will give them as much lifelong pleasure as the habit of reading.

Seedling Series is directed to elementary readers (grades 4-7), and **Student Series** is geared to junior and senior high school readers.

Our stories from all lands are carefully selected to promote and strengthen the reading habit.

Give a Harvest of the World's Best Short Stories
Published Four Times a Year for Growing Minds.

Please enter my subscription(s) to:
_____ **Seedling Series: Short Story International**
$16 U.S. & U.S. Possessions
Canada $19 (U.S.) All Other Countries $21 (U.S.)

_____ **Student Series: Short Story International**
$18 U.S. & U.S. Possessions
Canada $21 (U.S.) All Other Countries $23 (U.S.)

Mail with check to:
Short Story International
P.O. Box 405, Great Neck, New York 11022
Donor: Name_____
Address_____
City_____ State _____ Zip _____
Country _____

Send To: Name _____
Address _____
City_____ State _____ Zip _____
Country _____
Please check   ☐ *New Subscription*   ☐ *Renewal*

Send To: Name _____
Address _____
City_____ State _____ Zip _____
Country _____
Please check   ☐ *New Subscription*   ☐ *Renewal*